# REBEL REPRIEVE

## Hunter Dan

**Rebel Reprieve**
Copyright © 2019 by Hunter Dan

ISBN13: 978-1-7328729-4-3 (Paperback)
ISBN13: 978-1-7328729-5-0 (eBook)

Library of Congress Control Number: 2018964465

Printed in the United States of America

**Author Lair**
7220 N. Rosemead Boulevard, Suite 202-6,
San Gabriel, California, 91775

info@authorlair.com
www.authorlair.com

AUTHORLAIR

# Contents

# Dedication

It is an honor to dedicate this book to my two life long best friends since childhood. Jake Henne and Christopher Curtis whom we call Chris. It was their first names that gave me an identification for the main character Jake Christopher.

Jake lived next door to my family when I was adopted at 22 months old. Chris I have known since grade school. Our stories together really blossomed in our high school years. We have so many memories together to list but I would not trade my friendships with these guys. Our annual Red Sox trip 10 years strong has created some of the best memories.

Together we have stood behind one another. Cancer, Alcoholism and Vertigo have been no match as we all faced what could have torn us apart yet we conquered them having each other backs.

I am proud of who they have become. Beautiful wives and children who have grown into adults destined to make a difference in this world. They aren't just good friends, they are good husbands, fathers, sons and brothers.

I look forward to our future adventures. I love you both!

A special thank you to Jill Chase and Andy Bird for their technical support on this project. I couldn't have pulled this together without you!

# Chapter One

It is Friday morning, the last weekend in January. The alarm goes off at 6:00 A.M. as it had every weekday for the last six years. That will soon change as this is my last day of work. I was told a month ago that my sales position with the company had been eliminated due to budget cuts. I had a month to prepare for this day, and it feels like they just told me yesterday.

I was hoping after the horrible way last year ended that this year would be a big improvement. Horrible because in November my dad passed away. Even though Alzheimer's left him a shell of the man that he was, it's never easy saying goodbye to the man who adopted you when you were twenty two months old, provided you with a chance at the decent life, and saved you from bouncing from foster family to foster family. Ever since mom passed away five years ago, right before Jack, my nephew was born, dad and I became really close. And not only that, but two weeks before Christmas my girlfriend, Kayla, of three years informed me that a job opportunity on the west coast came up and was too good to pass up. She left the day after Christmas so that she could start her new job the day after New Year's Day.

What a coincidence she left the day after Christmas. Why, because on Christmas Eve while opening presents I was going to ask her to marry me. I had bought a ring to surprise her. However, the surprise was on me! I didn't tell her about it because she was so excited about her job opportunity. I had to support her decision. She was the best thing that ever happened to me. But who would I be if I left her deciding whether to stay or pass up the opportunity of a lifetime. After all, I still had the receipt. And, she promised to keep in touch. Was I wrong to hope things for her wouldn't work out? Not if I did it and kept it to myself. But as luck had it, she and her new employer are both very happy, so far.

So I lay here contemplating, do I get dressed and go to work on my last day? I won't accomplish anything on the job because really, who the hell cares. Or do I just say screw it and go AWOL. It didn't take me long to figure this one out. Really, who is going to blame me. I already have my two month severance check. So, as the sky prepared to lighten, I picked up the phone. Knowing if I call now I'll be able to leave a message on my boss's voice mail saying I won't be in today. I am going to start my new life, today. Everyone who knows me knows I am above going AWOL, and I wouldn't want to let anyone down. Or would I? Really, in just over two months I lost my father, my girlfriend and my job. I don't owe anybody a damn thing. Okay, I'm going to do this.

Three rings and the answering machine picks up. "Mr. Rodgers", I say nicely, "this is Jake. It's Friday morning and we both know it's my last day. I'm not going to lie to you. I appreciate everything you've done for me, but I won't be in today. I wouldn't have amounted to much, I would have had to say goodbye to everyone, and frankly, some people I didn't want to have to say goodbye. I don't know what I am going to do, I don't know where I am going to go, but I am going to do something for myself. I hope you are okay with this. By the time you get this message I will be headed somewhere." I said, "thanks for everything", and I hung up the phone.

I sat there feeling like a weight was lifted off my shoulders. I'm not sure why. After all, my dad is gone so I can't ask him "what would you do, dad"? My girlfriend is gone and it's 3:15 A.M. in California. I'd better not call her. Plus, I have no job. So whatever I do I don't have to answer to anyone, anything, or be anywhere any time soon.

So, before that weight even had a chance to come back, I lay on my bed, staring at the ceiling and try to prioritize the thoughts going through my head. I separated one idea I had from the rest. I turned on the news to determine if it was doable as far as the weather was concerned. After a few minutes the weather came on. With a fist pump of victory the meteorologist had confirmed my plan was meant to be. I wasted no time before I jumped out of bed, grabbed my suitcase and started packing like I had a time limit to get the hell out of Boston, point the tips of my skis north on I-93 and make my way to the snow capped Green Mountain state for a weekend getaway, a retreat. Hell, it's a Rebel Reprieve! I'm going to leave like I'm mad, I'm really not, but son of a gun, I'm going to act like I am.

I packed every necessity I could possibly need and maybe a few things I won't. But, something I grabbed that I think every car needs is a roll of toilet paper. You never know when Mother Nature or where Mother Nature will make that call. It's better to have it and not need it, than to need it and not have it. Somebody's famous last words I thought. Leaving the bedroom I glance at a picture of my dad with a stoic look on his face, and say, "see you soon dad."

As I load all my gear into my Beemer, I completed the process by locking my K2's and my poles on the ski rack on the roof.

I climb into the driver's seat, I open the sunroof interior cover so I can see up through the sunroof to spy on my skis to make sure they stay put. I'm paranoid like that. I give myself a last second quiz on my inventory. I went over it again. I looked at my watch. It's 7:15 A.M. I think to myself it's still pretty early. I can make good, goddamn time. I started my car and lowered my sunglasses from the brim of my Red Sox cap over my eyes, real serious-like. I said a little prayer that everyone will understand, but I realize the only thing that will upset them is I went alone and didn't tell anyone. They will get over it, I thought.

# Chapter Two

With the sun coming up, I turned left out of the driveway. I headed east right into the sun. I drive with barely any traffic at first, but when I drove by Northeastern, then the big fountain, the sun was finally shielded by the high rises as I head east on Huntington Avenue toward Chinatown and I-93.

With every light I pass by I get closer to the fresh air that will please my nostrils. I don't need to follow the signs, but I do just to be reminded of my purpose. I go sharp left, a few blocks, turn right and there it is. The entrance that leads me to the tunnel. I bear toward the north for the short stint through the tunnel, up past TD Garden, over the Bunker Hill Bridge with the tips of my skis cutting through the chilly air leading me to what I feel is going to be the best weekend I've had in years. At least this year I joke.

As I drive north I notice with every exit I drive by the traffic is getting thinner, and as I drive by I-95 North and South, there are by far fewer cars going North, and the Southbound lanes are bumper to bumper, barely moving. I thank them all for their participation in making my weekend escape possible and easy to get away with. I kind of feel bad for them, but I'll get over it. After all, who showed up for my pity party? Oh yeah,

I didn't have one. I decided not to stick around and hear all the sad goodbyes, the pats on the back and hugs from women who never really gave me the time of day for the last six years. Instead I'm leaving them wondering where could he possibly go, and what could he possibly be doing?

Well, that's for me to know, and me to not care if they ever find out. I'm out of the rat race and headed for my pace. I'm going to do what I want, when I want. I'm making the rules and the only one who can break them is me. Since I'm making this trip on my own with nobody to answer to for as long as I want and my Beemer gets me to Killington, I could care less.

As I glance at my speed I can't help but notice my gas gauge is near low and I really need some coffee. Even though it's the dead of winter, it doesn't slow down the construction any. There's always something going on at every exit or somewhere in between. One mile to Lowell and I-495 where I know I can get my gas and coffee without going astray too badly.

I pull into a station just off the exit. I will pump my gas, pull my car away from the pumps and go in and get a coffee. I do it that way instead of ignorantly leaving my car blocking the pumps for the next person. I may be on a Rebel Reprieve, but I don't have to be a jerk about it.

I may have grown up in the city, but I had compassion taught to me at an early age. I fill my tank then move to a parking spot and someone quickly moves up to pump gas. As I head in for a coffee, the guy who pulled up said "thanks for moving your car. Not very many people do these days." I smiled and said "I know, I drive a lot and I see all kinds." Some do, some don't. But I really felt good when the woman at the register thanked me for pulling up and parking. I smiled at her and said, "you are very welcome." I handed her a five for the coffee and she gave me the change. I headed for my car.

I turn up the radio and it's George Thorogood singing "I got a little change in my pocket going jingle lingle ling, want to call you on the telephone baby, I give you a ring." As I sing along in a good mood I realize I just got that change in my pocket and it's way too early to call Kayla. Not that I would.

# Chapter Three

I got back on I-93 with my tips once again headed northbound. I glance up and reassure myself they are still there. I never checked at the gas station. A few sips off my coffee and before I know it, I see the sign "Welcome to New Hampshire." The rest of the sign says "Live Free or Die", like there's no middle ground? Okay, I want to live free, and I'll stay up forever, I'll sleep when I'm dead, like my boss used to say.

I change the channel on the radio to Rock 101. I'll listen to Greg and the Morning Buzz as long as it comes in, or until 10:00 A.M. whichever comes first. But, since it's just after 8:00 A.M. I'll probably lose it first. I've listened to these guys for years. They are pretty hilarious. On comes Laura with the traffic update. I listen intuitively like my trip hinges on her every word, but she says nothing about I-93 northbound. Even though traffic is fairly heavy, we are moving right along. I wonder if she is as hot as she sounds? I have my mind made up that she is. I start picturing her in my mind, what could she look like? I say blonde, 5'4", nice build. I know from listening before she is pretty outgoing and adventurous, so she must be in pretty good shape. Okay, yeah, I'd love to meet her, but unless she is headed to Vermont skiing this weekend as well, then it's probably not going to happen. Not to mention, she's married and has a couple kids. Her husband is a lucky man.

I've decided I might as well stay in the left lane. Both lanes are pretty much bumper to bumper and whoever is in front of the left lane is barely moving faster than the right lane. So I'll just stay put. Anyway, I know for a fact once I get up past Exit 6 not only will a lot of cars go left, but we'll have several lanes to separate the men from the boys. As we get past mile marker 18 I see Exit 6 coming into view. My prediction looks to be right on. People in the left lane seem to be veering left, freeing up the flow continuing northbound.

I was never diagnosed with ADD, but my thoughts these last few miles have diverted reality from my mind. Meaning it's after 8:00 AM and I haven't received a call from my boss, which can mean one of two things - either he understands and is okay with my decision not to come to work, or he is so pissed at me and he chose not to call and vent his anger at me. I know I am hoping he is okay with it because there's no looking back now, and he accepts the fact that productivity was not high on my list of accomplishments for the day anyway. Neither was day-long goodbyes. When I come back I will call him. I'll say goodbye and if he is pissed, by then he will know telling me would not have changed anything. It is what it is. By then it will be "It was what it was."

I have now gone by 101 East. I'm going by Exit 9 North, then south past the cinemas, Home Depot and the sign "Last Exit Before Toll." My attention goes back to the radio and they announce Friday's weekly "punch-in-the-face." I draw a blank. What the hell! The only thing that comes to mind is how many people want to punch me in the face. I listen intently in hopes that nobody calls in and says "I'd like to punch my co-worker, Jake, for not showing up on his last day of work." Which, if someone did, I think Kelly Brown and Roadkill will have my back and with any luck the Godfather will see it my way as well.

The punches fly, my name isn't brought up, at least not yet. I turn the radio down a little to make my donation at the cash box because I've failed to see the need to get an E-Z Pass. The only time I wish I had one is now. I take my place in line to hand over my hard-earned money. It's the price you pay too, because now I have to roll down my window, smile, give them my buck and promise myself I'm going to get one, just not right now. Someday, then I won't even have to slow down.

I quickly roll up my window, turn the volume up, accelerate my X5 back up to speed as I glance up at my ski tips, still pointed north. I listen to the last punches and realize nobody is that mad at me. I sip my coffee and drive like I have somewhere to be. I fly by the rest area and liquor store in the hammer lane shaking my head. Why? Well, in a society that is so hell bent against drinking and driving, they put a liquor store on the side of a super highway that makes anyone who wasn't ever thinking about drinking think about drinking. Like this coffee would be better if I pour some Kahluha in it. Not that I would, but since it's right there and it opens in 20 minutes at 9:00 A.M., I could spice things up a little. But knowing how far I still have to go, the big boy in me says, "Jake, don't even think about it." So I listen to my wiser sub-conscience and turn my attention back to the only buzz allowed on this journey, that's the Buzz on the radio.

Only god knows how many people buy a bottle here and crack it before they even get up to speed. I guess I don't get the logic. Must be the State knows their booze is cheaper so they will take chances to make a buck on out-of-staters who only pulled in to go use the restroom.

So as I put that bull behind me, I take a couple more sips off my coffee and gear up for the junction ahead that will put me on I-89 North and sixty miles from the Vermont border. It feels like my coffee is getting low, so I weigh my options. I could stop here in Bow and get gas-station coffee, or I can go 20 miles north on I-89 and stop in Warner at the Irving and get a coffee at Dunkin' Donuts. I shook my cup, gauge my bladder and decide we are good until Warner. So I merge into the I-89 north lane and past Pitco Frialator onto I-89 north. Again I glance up and the K2's are still pointed toward White River Junction. Yeah, baby, now the sun went from my right side and now is behind me.

I adjust my Sox cap and sunglasses again as if I'm settling in for the duration. I settle into my safe haven and check my mirrors becoming aware of who and what is around me. I check my watch and immediately gauge the time in California and decide that I'll text Kayla when I stop for gas. She'll be up by then, and out of respect for my sis, I will let Anne know I didn't go to work. I'll tell her I'm going to get away skiing for the weekend and will check in when I get back.

That being said, I head for my next cup of coffee. As the miles click away my bladder reminds me not to lally gag as that is priority number one when I get to Warner. And with every mile it speaks louder and more clear.

As I get to the exit my need to go is high. My savior is in sight as I get to the stop sign. I go left, into the round-about and steer into the Irving. I pull into a parking spot in front of the door. My pace is quick as I head toward the back of the store to the men's room. Awww, the relief, it's just that. I wash my hands, exit the restroom and get in line at Dunkin' Donuts. As I wait I look out the window. The car next to mine has its hood up and a man is staring at the engine.

I hear a soft voice say, "May I help you?"

I turn around and realize she is talking to me. I step up and announce, "I'll have a large Turbo hot, cream and sugar and an extra shot of espresso."

"A second shot of espresso"?, she asks.

I say, "Yes, the shot that comes with it and another on top of that making two shots." I say that so we are on the same page. I watch as they put in the espresso. One shot goes in, then the second shot. She then pours in the coffee, cream and sugar. She puts the cup down and rings it up and asks for $3.69. The price varies from store to store, but that's about right. I pay with my debit card, slide the receipt into my wallet. As always, I walk up to the napkin and straw holder. I take two napkins and put them over the cover of my coffee, flip it upside down twice to stir the cream and sugar. They don't stir anything at Dunkin' Donuts. They make it and give it to you. I learned how to do that from a DD employee in Hoosick, New York.

I went outside and I got back in my car. I notice the gentleman next to me still looking under his hood. He is dressed in a suit and has a nice car. I think to myself he isn't just checking his oil. Then I remember to text Kayla. "Morning, sweetheart, I didn't go to work. I'm heading away to enjoy myself for the weekend. I miss you and wish you were here. Hope all is well (even though I really don't). I will call you later. Love you!"

Then I send a message to Anne. "Hi sis. I said screw it and didn't go to work today. My last day and I wouldn't have accomplished anything anyway. I'm taking off for the weekend. TTYL."

I put my phone down, take a sip of my coffee and the guy is still standing in front of his car, hood still up, and I see his breath from the cold air as he talks on his cell phone. I faintly hear him say "I'll get there as quick as I can."

My curiosity gets the best of me, so I roll down my window and say "what's wrong with your car?"

He said "I'm not sure, but it's not running right. I have a meeting to be at 10:00", he added.

Of course I had to ask, "where's the meeting?"

"At the VA in White River Junction", he said. I looked at my watch. It's 9:15 A.M. I think to myself that I can give him a ride and get him to his meeting on time if he leaves his car. So the good Samaritan in me announces this to him and he looks amazed.

I said "do you have Triple A?", and he said he did.

Then he said "really, you will give me a ride to White River?"

"Sure, I'm going right through it, it's no problem", I say. I recommended he move his car so Triple A will be able to pick it up easily as well as find it. So he did. He grabbed his briefcase, jacket, sunglasses and a box. He placed a call to Triple A. Then he went into the store to warn the clerk they will be picking up his car.

He got in and said "okay, I think I'm ready. By the way, my name is Tim, Tim Chandler."

"Nice to meet you, Tim. My name is Jake, Jake Christopher." We shook hands and I put my X5 in reverse and headed for the on-ramp.

# Chapter Four

Just to get some conversation going, I asked Tim, "so, what do you do for work?"

Tim explains "well, Jake, I'm a marketing rep for a company that makes replacement knees. We manufactured the first replacement knee that is durable enough to run on."

"Run on?", I asked, "you mean they don't already have them in existence?"

"No, the ones on the market up until now aren't durable enough to run on. As a matter of fact, they only last about ten years. We now have a product that can be a replacement on a 50 year old person and not only can they be running in just a couple of months, but they could live to be 85 years old and never need a new knee", Tim said.

Amazed and grateful for my healthy knees, I begin to praise his occupation, because I know a couple of people who have had knees replaced. But, not having knee problems myself, it's hard to comprehend the disability and suffering of one who needs a new knee.

He continues "I am on my way to the VA to introduce our prototype to the orthopedic surgeons there, as well as some doctors from Dartmouth-Hitchcock. This meeting is so important to our company. It's never a good time when you have car trouble, but some times are truly worse than others. I am really grateful for the ride, Jake."

"Now that you know where I'm headed", he said, "where are you headed? If you don't mind my asking. Obviously my guess is you're going skiing."

"Yes, sir", I said, "I'm headed to Killington for the weekend, maybe longer if I feel like staying since I really have no reason to be anywhere Monday or Tuesday, or the whole week for that matter." Tim was a bit puzzled and inquired why I answered a little sarcastically.

"Well", I explained, "I lost my job, my dad passed away in November, and my girlfriend landed a job in California at the first of the year. My sales job was eliminated due to budget cuts, and today was my last day, only I didn't go in. Instead I packed my car and I'm headed to spend some of my severance pay skiing in Vermont."

"I hear you, man", Tim said, "I don't blame you a bit. I applaud your decision and respect the move given the streak of bad luck you have been dealt. You know what they say, God has a plan." I was quick to say "well His plan for me is enough to make or break a man." Tim just smiled and nodded his head and agreed.

As they neared the New London exit, mile marker 40, we agree it's 20 miles to the border of Vermont, so our ETA at the VA is at about 9:55 A.M. "Five minutes before the meeting.

I won't be there as early as I would have liked, but under the circumstances, I'm lucky to make it at all", Tim said.

As they continue to chew up the miles, Tim says, "I wish I could have bought you that coffee, Jake."

"That's okay, I say, "You were busy with your car. I was there to get one, and to get rid of one."

As we descend into Grantham, I look out to the left lifting my sunglasses and say "I love looking at the snow covered rocky top of Corbin Mountain over there."

Tim agrees "It sure is beautiful. I think that's a private game preserve", he adds.

In trying to keep the conversation alive, I ask "where are you from?"

"I'm from Manchester", Tim says.

"Do you have any family?", I ask looking at his left hand for a ring. Tim holds up his left hand bearing his wedding ring.

"Yes, I am married and have two kids. A boy and a girl. I'm originally from Nashua. I went to UNH and I met my wife there my senior year. We married a few years later. My son is five and my daughter is three. They both are beautiful kids", he explains.

All of a sudden Tim says, "I need to call my wife to tell her about the car. And, damn, I need to call my boss, too. I have to make arrangements on how I am going to get back home. They said my car was being towed to the dealership in Bow."

So Tim pulled out his phone and called his wife. "Hi, honey, my car broke down on the way to the meeting. I had to have it towed. I have a ride to the VA. I'll just make it on time. Yes, I'm okay, he said, "I was lucky enough that the guy parked next to me was going through White River and offered to give me a ride. Yes, the car was towed to Bow, I'll check on it after the meeting and will call you. I love you too, babe. I'll check back with you later. Bye, sweetie." He looked at me and smiled. He said "she is awesome. I don't know how I got so lucky." As he dialed again I looked at my watch, it said 9:40 A.M. I couldn't help but think of Kayla and what our lives would have been like as husband and wife and living the dream.

As that thought danced around in my head, Tim began to speak. It sounds as though he's leaving a message. He said "Good morning, Mr. White. It's Tim. My car broke down on the way to White River. I have a ride and will be at the meeting on time. My ETA is 9:55 A.M., not as early as I had planned, but I called the VA and they know when I'll be arriving. I'll call you back after the meeting." He looked at his watch and said "if you get this message in the next 15 minutes, give me a call, otherwise I'll talk to you later. I need a ride, my car was towed to Bow. I'll check on it later and I'll get back to you if I don't hear from you, thanks." And he hung up. He took a deep breath, paused and said to me, "He'll call if he gets it before the meeting, he's a good man to work for. He will most likely foot the bill for the tow and repair. He takes care of his employees and knows how to run a business. You never see him get angry." He checks his watch again as we go by Exit 16. He looks at me and says "we're going to make it", as a smile crosses his face.

I think to myself, he's got a wife he adores, two kids, and the American dream. He has a great job, works for a good company with a bright future and a boss that he speaks highly of. I can't help but envy his life. It seems he's done well for himself, college education to boot. That thought crosses my mind as we approach Exit 17 with a bit heavier traffic ahead. I'm not sure I should say anything to Tim, but I do anyway. "I've got to hand it to you, Tim, you have a good thing going. You're happily married, two kids, good job. Do your parents still live around here?"

And it was like a lightbulb lit up in his head. He grabbed his phone again and said "thanks, Jake, I'll call my dad, he will probably drive to White River and pick me up. That's perfect!" He dials again and his dad picked up. He explains what happened and it wasn't like he was talking to his dad. It sounded more like he was talking to a friend and asked him for a ride. And, not just across town. I don't think his dad batted an eyelash. I clearly could hear him say "Sure. You're at the VA in White River. That's only an hour and a half away. I can be there at noon." Before Tim hung up the phone he said "Thanks, dad. I love you. I'll see you then." Another smile gleamed across his face. He looked at me and said "thanks, Jake. You nailed that one. And to answer your question, my parents still live in Nashua in the house I grew up in."

As the border is almost in sight, we approach Exit 20 and Tim says "My boss will be happy my dad is coming to get me. Plus, it gives my dad something to do. He just retired last year and tries to keep busy. But this will get him out of the house, out of my mom's hair and give him something to do. He likes to help people. I guess that's why he delivers Meals on Wheels a couple of days a week."

As we pass over the Connecticut River and into Vermont Tim's phone rings. He picks it up and says "hello", he paused "Hi, Mr. White", he said. Another pause, "yeah, I'm not sure what's wrong with the car. I had it towed to the dealership in Bow. I'll be at the VA in a minute, and my dad will be here at noon to pick me up. I've got everything I need. I'll see how the car is on the way down. If it's not ready, my dad can bring me to the office." As he listened he nodded his head a couple of times and I could tell he was being humble as he received praise from the other end. He ended up saying "yes, sir. I'm ready and I'll call you when the meeting is over." He paused and ended by saying "thank you, sir. I'll talk to you soon" as he hung up.

I was turning into the driveway of the VA and saw a huge "Welcome Veterans" sign lit up. I headed up the hill and looked at my watch. It said 9:53 A.M. We were right on schedule. As we approached the front door, Tim reached for his wallet. I said "I don't want any money. It was on my way anyway, and it's my pleasure to have met you."

He reached in his wallet and handed me a business card and said "call me. I would love to hear about your ski trip." With that he opened the door, grabbed his stuff out of the back seat and quickly said "thanks again, Jake, I owe you." He smiled, closed the door and quickly walked inside.

# Chapter Five

I felt this connection and a warm, but good, feeling like everything that I lost in the last few months he had and he knew what to do with it, but really didn't realize it because he hadn't lost any of it. Kind of hard to explain, but that thought is in my head and I don't have to explain it to anyone.

As I sat there I turned on my GPS because now I'm slightly off course and I need to get back on track. There, it's all set. At the bottom of the hill it's telling me to go right .2 tenths of a mile, then right on the VA Cutoff Road. As I approach the gate at the bottom of the drive to the VA, I see a Dunkin' Donuts across the street. I pull in and park. I then run in, use the restroom, grab a coffee and a bagel and get back in the car. I follow the directions on the GPS to the VA Cutoff Road, which then takes me to Route 4 and tells me to go left. Now I am on the road that takes me to Killington and I soon drive by the exit where I would have gotten off had I not brought Tim to the VA.

All of a sudden the silence registers in my mind and I think the Greg and the Morning Buzz program is over. I realize as I turn up the radio that Rock 101 is no more. So I hit the search button and it quickly stops on 100.5. A country song is playing and I think to myself, not in my car, not today, I'm not in the mood for country. A song will come on and just kill the positive vibes that brighten my mood right now. I hit the search button again and it stops on 99.3. That's better, but search again, 98.1, again 97.1 - no way, 95.3 ugh, country again; 93.9, one more, 92.3. Yeah, bingo! It's a girl DJ, and all I heard her say was Daughtry. That's perfect! I can crank this and sing it with him. I know it word-for-word. I have the CD, I think to myself, but I haven't heard it in quite a while, and Home is my favorite song from him.

I take a sip of my coffee and unwrap my bagel. I take a couple of bites as I drive past Quechee Gorge Village. I adjust my hat and glasses. Even though it's the middle of winter, you never know when a pedestrian will step out of nowhere to see the Gorge. The radio is cranking Daughtry, the sun at my back, and my bagel on the passenger seat. I reach over to grab the half I started and chow down as I work my way west. The other half is loaded with cream cheese. As I finish that, I reach a reduce speed sign as I come into Woodstock. I look in the rear view mirror for stray cream cheese on my goatee.

I spy on the die-hard shoppers who flock to this town and walk around with their steaming cups of coffee window shopping at 10:30 in the morning. The women duck into an occasional shop seemingly to warm up as their man follows suit, most likely to open the door like a gentleman would do. Kayla had me stop here once so I can relate to the guys. But God forbid if I would let her talk me into spending the night here. It is just as expensive as staying on the mountain with none of the nightlife. So as fast as I came into this town, I am headed out the other side.

As I pass the high school, my foot wants to get heavy. As I leave the school zone and see the 40 mile per hour sign, I push it a bit and see I'm doing 50 miles per hour. See ya, suckers, I say to the guys in my rearview mirror and head for the hills like the man on a mission who left Boston some three hours ago.

Before I know it, I'm coming into Bridgewater where 25 miles per hours means it, not 26 or 27 miles per hour. Just ask the county mounty. What county mounty? The one you are about to encounter at any point as you pass through this town. No stop lights or stop signs. Just speed limit signs that should say obey or pay. The police log is 98% traffic tickets. The other 2% is probably animal complaints. I could stop at Long Trail Brewery, but that bagel will get me to Killington. And, I would be tempted to have an IPA. I can wait until I get to my destination. Plus, when I get there I have to find a room. So right now I'm not sure of my destination. I just know I'm only 20 minutes away. My ETA is 11:00 A.M., ironically the same time people need to check out. So I'll just look for vacancy signs as I drive up the Access Road.

Now I've passed the brewery and the IPA, although it may have sounded good, the coffee too will get me to Killington. Which reminds me, my bladder is now getting more exercise than anything and tells me it doesn't belong to a trucker, its more like a little kid asking "are we there yet?" So of course I'm not going to answer. I know that I can't go any faster than the car in front of me. I drive through this cornery canyon that reminds me of the Valley of the Dinosaurs. At one time it probably was! But before I know it I've exited the Corners and am going by Route 100 and the old Back Behind Saloon.

The most familiar sight will be the cat walk-over Route 4 and the gondolas. That tells me I am close, so close. Two miles of straightaway to the base of the big hill. As we reach the straightaway I tell my bladder, "hang on, we're staying behind this car." If I pass him, I'd probably get a speeding ticket and where will that leave me. After Goodro Lumber and I reach the hill, there's a passing lane. I'll show him how to get a move-on. Although, I may not be able to hold it until I find a room, at least I'll get to the Access Road.

With the passing lane in sight, my bladder tells my right foot what to do, and it listens as my X5 kicks it up a notch and leaves them behind like they were standing still. I'm staying in the left lane since I'll need to be here to take a left up the Access Road. As I crest the hill and see the Killington sign, I am reminded to turn on my blinker.

# Chapter Six

I am here I think to myself. It's like another weight just lifted and calmed my nerves. I am about to have a great weekend after I find a place to relieve myself. Although I always say all I need is a tree, I quickly see a construction site with two portables right next to the job trailer. I pull in, drive up to them and park. I hop in one of them like it was a desert oasis and like I had every right to use it. I get back in my car. As I round the corner I see the Summit Lodge sign on the left. I look up and there it is, not another oasis, but my Rebel Reprieve playground staring down at me, like the Abominable Snowman on Rudolf the Red Nosed Reindeer stared down at those intimidated by his presence. Only difference is I'm not scared of that hill. I'm here to tame it and ski it as if it were a Mustang that needed to be broken in. As I get closer I see two peaks. Just then I look up at my skis and see two tips that say K2. One set of K2s that will own the two K2s that draw them closer as if they were magnetized.

As I continue past the famous Pickle Barrel, I reminisce about the time I saw Tesla play there. What a show! I look at the sign to see who is playing tonight as I continue passing by. I think that will be my destination tonight, but first I need to find a bed I'll be able to crash in after a night on the town. I didn't quite see the sign. I think it said Jason something. There's the Wobbly Barn, good food, fun atmosphere. And it hits me. I've been here so many times but this time is different. I have never been here by myself. It will be a different experience for sure. "Will I be okay?", I ask myself. I don't see why not. I'm a people person.

Up ahead I see the Basin Ski Shop. It reminds me that my skis need tuning, so I stop to see if they can tune them up this afternoon. I hurry through the door and head right to the tuning counter as I've done before.

"Hey man, what are the chances you could tune my skis at some point today?", I ask.

He checks the clock and replies "I can do them right after lunch, can you leave them?" I said "sure, no problem. I'll go get them."

I excuse myself and do an about-face out to my car. I grab my skis and hurry back in out of the frigid temps. The dude hands me a tag to fill out. He hands me a stub from the tag and said "they'll be done around 2:00 P.M., but you might want to call first just in case."

I said "no problem. I'll go find a room for the weekend."

"Find a room?", he said. "You don't have a reservation?"

"No", I replied. "It's kind of a long story, but I'm here a little spontaneously. I'm by myself. I'll find something."

The guy behind the counter says "good luck."

Off I went in quest of a room. I continued up the Access Road and turned left onto East Mountain Road. The Fountain Inn sign says "No Vacancy" so I continue on.

On the left I see the Mountain Green. Not seeing any sign, I decide to check the Grand. I pull in and see a bellhop outside. I ask if there are any rooms available for the weekend. His reply was a combination of surprise and smart-aleck when he said "no sir, we are booked for the weekend." I didn't even have to get out of my car.

So I headed back up to check out the Mountain Green and as I pull in I look over at the Fountain Inn sign. The sign said "Vacancy", and just two minutes ago it said "No Vacancy." So I quickly drove over, parked my car and went in.

I walk up to the counter and this very pretty young lady looks up and says "May I help you?"

I said "yes, I see the sign says vacancy. I'm looking for a room for tonight and tomorrow night."

She replied "your timing is impeccable. I just had a cancellation."

I replied "I know. I went by a few minutes ago and the sign said no vacancy. I checked the Grand and came back up and saw your sign said vacancy."

She said "it's a single queen, no smoking, $189.00 a night, plus tax."

I said without hesitation, "I'll take it for two nights." I handed her my credit card and before I know it she says "sign here." She then handed me a receipt, a parking pass and a room key. She said "you'll probably want to park out back. Your key will open the outside door and it's the second room on the left, Room 103."

I notice the restaurant's name is the Santa Cruz Steakhouse. I ask if the restaurant is worth checking out? The young girl at the desk assured me the food is very good. I really wanted to ask if she would join me for dinner, but I held back and did the gentlemanly thing and just said, "thanks for the recommendation." I smiled to see if she smiled back. She did and as quickly as I checked her left ring finger, I grabbed my key, put my receipt in my wallet and headed out to move in. I thought to myself maybe she is working tomorrow and maybe I'll work up the nerve to ask her out. After all, I really haven't dated since Kayla left and she was pretty enough to allow myself a second chance!

I now have my room. I have two hours to move in and kill before I call Basin to check on my skis. I get in my car and drive around the back and park in front of the door. It says "no parking" but I'm sure it's okay to unload and then move to another spot. There is a handicap spot next to this one. But I'm not surprised nobody is parked there. Probably no one ever parks there I thought.

# Chapter Seven

I unload my bags and carry them in. I grab my boots and poles and go through the door quickly. I didn't want to annoy anyone with my ignorance to the cold, or what may appear to be ignorance to someone else. Now everything is in the room so I move my car halfway back out to the road. I set the alarm, locked it and checked the doors to be sure, thinking I may leave it there for the duration of my stay. Before I get back to the door I remembered I have to go back and get my skis. Oh well, I'll just reset the alarm. I went back into my room and began to unpack. My ski clothes I laid out on the couch; my dress shirts and pants I hung up between the bathroom door and the room door. My bathroom stuff I laid out on the sink.

Now that I was done unpacking I turned on the television to see what I have for channels. I don't imagine I'll watch much television. After all, I am here to ski and party, but I am a guy so you never know when you can catch a Bruins or Celtics game. Or, if I want to see what the weather will be like. It seems it's a very basic package looking at the channel guide.

Last, but not least, I have one last thing to check out. I peeled back the quilt from the bed, then the blanket and the sheets. I lifted the mattress off the box spring and peered between them.

Okay, I am satisfied they don't exist here. I put the bed back together with no sign of bedbugs. Relieved, I tuck the sheets back in, complete with the blanket and quilt. I am grateful. I don't know how I could have gone back to the front desk and announced to the pretty young woman that I found bedbugs. After all, that would have been a complete deal breaker for me, and I don't even want to think of how she'd have reacted.

I still have an hour to kill before I call on my skis. So I surf for the Weather Channel to get the forecast for the weekend. As luck would have it, they have the regular networks and a selection of specialty channels like ESPN, TBS, TNT, Lifetime, History and yes, the Weather Channel.

The Weather Channel finally gets to the northeast, but as usual, which I've never minded before, when they talk Northeast, they mention Boston! I'm not sure if they know Vermont and New Hampshire actually exist, or that a forecast for Boston means nothing to those flocking out of the rat race to a weekend retreat at a place not that far away. Whatever the weather in Vermont isn't necessarily the same as in Boston.

Fortunately, as they talk about Boston the local forecast is displayed across the bottom of the screen. Overall, it looks like mostly sunny all weekend; below freezing at night so they should be able to make snow; mid-30s during the day. There may be possible snow Sunday night. Since I just arrived, I'll look at Sunday as a world away. However, since I'm on a ski weekend, snow is not a reason to panic, unless I'm driving in it. If I leave Sunday there will have to be a reason, but right now I don't have one. This morning I listened to the Boston forecast. Again, the only way I could believe this was the same forecast was if we were in for a Nor'Easter, and I haven't heard that from anybody.

While I still have 45 minutes to kill, I'm starting to get a little hungry. I put on my jacket and head out to the car and head down the hill past the Basin where my skis are being tuned up. As I drive by the Killington Mountain school I turn on my left blinker and pull into the Phat Italian. Inside the front door, maybe two steps, my nose decides what I'm having. Pizza! I walk over to the warmer where I can grab pizza by the slice. I grab two pieces of what looks like the works and grab a Coke from the cooler. I walk over to the register and pay for it. Now I can sit in my car and eat it or sit at one of those little tables over there. I want to sit and enjoy my food so I go sit at one of the tables. I sit so I can see what's going on in the store, not because I'm nosy, but I just want to enjoy the goings on as I am here by myself. And you never know, maybe I'll see someone else who is on their own Rebel Reprieve. I think, really, what are the chances of that?

Instead, I'm just as content determining locals or out-of-stater. Well, it's not long before the first piece is gone, and the locals are in the lead at the register. It's easy to tell. I can tell by how they are dressed and how they interact with the guy at the register, and not so much by their interaction, but by the reaction of the young man at the register. He treats the locals like they are friends of his, as they probably are. And, the visitors just pay for their stuff with no conversation and barely a smile. I would rather be treated like a local. The way to be treated that way is to treat them the way I want to be treated. It's a no-brainer. It doesn't happen like that in the city. People are much more reserved as if they are afraid that everyone is trying to rip them off. Then it dawns on me, I had walked up, paid for my stuff, and didn't engage in conversation either. Under my own observation, I am classified as a flatlander.

I take a big swig of my soda, wipe my mouth, take a deep breath and check my watch. Its 1:55 P.M. I have to go by the ski shop so I'll stop in and see if they are ready. I sit here for another minute to take in more of this Vermont life. After all, I don't have to be there right at 2:00 P.M., and I really don't need to call. I take one last sip of my soda, throw my plate and napkins in the rubbish and head out to my car. As I approach it I unlock it, get in, start it and head up the road.

After about a half mile I veer into the Basin parking lot. I check to make sure I have my ticket and head to the front door. The dude who tuned my skis grabbed them and said "$45.00 will do it. Did you find a room?"

"Yep, at the Fountain Inn", I said. Just then an older gentleman with a name tag that said Rick butted in and said "That's a loud rocking motel. I hope you like to party."

"Sounds good to me", I said, "I'm looking for some excitement." I hand him the $45.00 in cash and say, "thanks, bud."

He said "you're very welcome, have a great weekend!"

As I walked away I turned and answered "that's my plan," with a smile and headed toward the door. I loaded the skis and headed back to my room.

I parked out back, locked my car and headed to my room. I checked the time, 2:15 P.M. I think to myself, what do I do now. You know, I don't know how tonight will go so I'll take a nap. I woke up at 6:00 A.M. and probably will stay out late, so a little nap will do me some good.

I take my clothes off, pull back the covers and slide on in. I lay there wondering, what did Mr. Rodgers think? Are my co-workers pissed? What does Kayla think? What does Anne think? How did Tim's meeting go? Did his dad make it to

White River to get him? Jesus, how am I going to sleep with all that running through my head, I say to myself.

I decided to do a little meditation to clear my mind. I say to myself "I am that, I am, I am that, I am. I am happy, I am. I am happy, I am." I say it a few more times and change to tired. "I am tired, I am. I am tired, I am." This helps clear my mind. I keep repeating it to convince my mind that I am tired. I fall asleep much faster by clearing out the questions, all those people, and convince my mind and body to shut down and relax. "I am tired, I am. I am tired, I am." As I am completely relaxed the last thing I remember is steady breathing and feeling at peace.

# Chapter Eight

The next thing I know my eyes open and the room is completely dark. I look at the clock. It says 5:30. Shocked a bit my mind immediately says in the evening or morning. I slept pretty well but I couldn't have slept through the night. I turn on the television to CBS where it confirms my intuition. It's the CBS evening news. So I lay there and watch the news for a bit. As the cobwebs clear from my brain I laugh and say, "you dummy, there's no way you slept for 15 hours."

After just a few minutes the weather comes on. Now this forecast is out of Burlington Vermont so it's quite a bit more believable given its proximity. Although it's similar to what I had seen earlier, I feel much better about this forecast. Saturday will be a good day to ski, as well as Sunday with snow moving in late Sunday.

I haven't even stepped in my skis and I'm already thinking of staying Sunday night riding out the storm and skiing fresh powder on Monday. But, again it's Friday and I want to enjoy this trip one second, one minute, one hour, one day at a time. So Monday at this point is a long way off.

I turn on the television to VH1 for the music and it's John Mayer's video with Taylor Swift "Can't Stop Loving You." That was Kayla's and my song together. I sit there and watch the video and can't help but reminisce about the best thing I ever had and let get away.

When the video is over I pick up my phone and send her a text simply saying "I love you!" Knowing it's 2:45 P.M. in California, I'm not sure when she will get it, but I know she will respond at some point, whether she is at work or not.

I grab a towel and head into the bathroom to take a shower. I pull back the shower curtain and turn on the water. I turn the shower handle all the way to hot and turn it back toward cold to get it to my liking.

When I was done drying off I look in the mirror. It's pretty fogged up and say to myself "If anyone can do this, it's you." My curiosity got the best of me. I look at my phone and sure enough Kayla responded. "I love you, too. What are you doing?" I quickly typed out, "I went away for a couple of days." As I prepared to go out she responded "Okay. Be careful. I miss you a lot." I responded "I miss you, too. I think about you all the time." She came right back, "same here." As I get dressed and brush my teeth I can't help but think Kayla bought these pants and this shirt. I'm going to look good thanks to her.

Just then my new neighbors whom I haven't seen, seem to be getting along very well at the moment. I do believe they are getting it on. She is agreeable with what he is doing and "yes" is what she is repeatedly saying quite loudly. As they progress so does the noise. The bed is squeaking and the headboard is banging back and forth against the wall between our rooms.

I turn up the volume on the television to drown out the sounds of love. I grab my phone and jokingly send Kayla a text bragging in envy about my faceless neighbors. "Are you jealous?", she asked. "Damn right", I said. "I told you I wish you were here. We could give them a taste of their own medicine. I had to turn the television up." Back she came with an LOL and a smiley face!

I wish she were here because this is hard to take. But since she has been gone for a month, I will most likely do what I've done for the whole month of January. Not that that's the only time I've taken care of myself, but for the last month it has gotten me by. I guess Rick at the Basin was right, this is a rocking party motel.

Things now have come to a halt next door so I am thinking they have brought this one in for a landing. As it is nearing 6:30 P.M., I let Kayla know they are finished and I am headed for dinner and after that a stiff drink. If I smoked I would go out and have a butt, but thank God I quit that before I ever got started. I'll leave that up to them. She did sound a little raspy like a smoker, I thought.

As I contemplated it was Kayla and I, I heard their door shut. Curiosity has overcome me and I said screw it. I'm heading for dinner so I can get a glimpse of them or her as I want to put a face with the sound of what I just heard. Hopefully it's just her I say to myself as I grab my room key and phone.

I go into the hallway and sure enough I see a woman going out the door with a cigarette and lighter in her hand. As she pushed open the door she looked back and smiled at me and exited as if she knew exactly what my intention was. That all happened so fast I didn't even get a chance to return a smile. I just turned left to go down the hall to the short set of stairs that leads up to the main lobby and to the entrance of the Santa Cruz.

I say to myself "I called that." Now the fact that she's a smoker does nothing for me, but she is attractive and I was able to put a face with the sounds of love. After all, I really hadn't heard her say anything other than "yes, yes, yes." That's not considered a sentence. Maybe I'll get a better look at her later. They must be here for the weekend.

# Chapter Nine

I climb the stairway to the lobby. I glance at the front desk and I am not surprised that the young woman at the front desk is nowhere to be seen. I walk into the Santa Cruz and this young woman says "are you here to meet someone, or are you by yourself?"

"Well I'm afraid I'm here by myself", I reply.

She said "you can sit at the bar if you would like, or Amanda will be right back and she can seat you at a table." I started to say I'll seat myself at the bar, but before I even completed saying I will, I look up and there she is, it was her. Amanda is the girl from the front desk this morning. I scramble for a second with my thoughts, but I am able to say I would like to sit at a table.

"Alright, please follow me", Amanda said with a menu in her hand. As she led me into the dining room she said as she looked back with a smile, "you decided to take me up on my recommendation."

I said "you remember me"? She said, "of course. Your name is Jake. You checked in today taking over the reservation that was canceled." As we get to my table she said "will this be okay? It's the last table we have that only seats two."

I said "it will be fine." "So you work here in the restaurant too? Why didn't you tell me that when I asked about the restaurant?"

She replied "You asked me how the food was and I answered your question." She smiled, placed my menu in front of me and said "your server will be over in just a minute."

"Okay, thank you. It's too bad you couldn't join me."

"Well, she said, "I only work in the restaurant on Thursday and Friday nights. I know you booked for two nights. I may be free tomorrow night."

"Will you be working the front desk tomorrow?", I ask.

"From 8:00 A.M. until 4:00 P.M. I will", she said. "I have Sunday and Monday off."

Right now I'm not worried about tomorrow. I have her in my sights again and I'm not going to let her slip out of my radar this time. So I said before she walked away "do you have any plans after you get out of work?"

She had a surprised look and glanced up with a half smile on her face. "When I get out of work?", she asked. "I kind of have plans. My friend and I talked about going to either the Pickle or the Wobbly for a drink."

I quickly filled her in that I planned on going out later, but hadn't made a decision where yet. My waitress arrived and is waiting to introduce herself. So I said to my hopefully-soon-to-be friend "I'll stop and see you after my dinner if that's okay with you?"

"Okay", she said and turned and headed back toward the entrance.

My attention went to the waitress who patiently waited for my conversation to end. "My name is Molly, I will be your server tonight", she said. As she rattled off the specials, I was thinking what do I want to drink. When she finished her well-rehearsed list, she asked what I wanted to drink.

"I would like a stiff Jack and Ginger, please. It's been a long day, I mention. "I'll get that for you and give you a chance to look over the menu", she said.

As I studied the menu I felt I was taking an open book Mexican quiz. I have no idea what any of these dishes are, but the definitions are written after all of them so idiots like myself can learn some Spanish, and maybe look halfway intelligent. It's all in the pronunciation.

As I narrow it down to a couple of familiar names, I decide on a beef chimichanga with rice and a salad as Molly returned with my special guests, Jack and Ginger. She placed it in front of me and asked if I was ready to order.

I said, "sure, I'll have the beef chimichanga with rice and a salad.

She asks, "what kind of dressing would you like."

I said, "thousand island."

She nodded, smiled and said "sure thing."

As she went to place my order I toasted to my journey, my trip that I had no idea I would be doing when I woke up this morning. Now it seems like things could be falling into place. As I took another sip I looked up and there was Amanda walking by me to seat another table. As my lips touched my glass I believe she smiled as she looked at me while going by. Even though she caught me off guard, the feeling I got from that smile was warmer than the Jack Daniels was that was coating the intestinal highway to my stomach.

As I look around the restaurant I feel a little strange. I am the only person that is sitting alone. Now unlike this afternoon in the Phat Italian, I was able to pick apart the tourists from the locals. In here at dinner, I guarantee all the patrons are tourists. The only locals are the staff. And I bet half of the staff aren't from around here, including Amanda. But do I really care who is who, where anybody is from, or what brings them here on this week? All that matters is what brings me here. Nobody knows my story and that is the reason why I had to get away. To be by myself to rediscover or reinvent who I want to be. And to do what makes me feel alive and happy. Even though I am here alone, I don't have to be alone.

As I continue to sip my drink, I look up again at the lovely Amanda who was walking toward me to seat another couple. As they approached I notice it's my smoking neighbor. As she stopped two tables away she makes eye contact and smiles at me. I smile and nod as if in approval to what we both know. And for him, I bet her husband knows nothing as there is really nothing to know. His wife knows I am staying next to them. She has smiled at me twice, but that is hardly a reason for him to be upset, I think to myself.

As I watch them get seated by Amanda, I notice her husband's back is to me. She is facing me in clear view. I turn my attention to my drink and find my sips have turned to gulps. As I now don't know how to feel, I gather Molly's attention. She approaches my table and I order another Jack and Ginger. While I wait I look around the room and catch myself checking out the neighbor couple. Something about her intrigues me. I'm not sure if it's her smile, the way she sounded during their sexcapade, or the fact that she is sending me interesting signals as we both continue to make eye contact.

As Molly delivers my new drink, she informs me my dinner will be right out. Before I can even get a sip of my new drink, my dinner arrives being delivered by a young lady I hadn't seen before now. As she puts my plate in front of me I say, jokingly, "that's not what I ordered!" The look on her face was that of surprise and confusion. I quickly said "I'm just kidding", to her to let her off the hook and relax, as she must be fairly new and working hard to do a good job. I don't want to be the cause of a meltdown.

She smiled and said "I totally believed you!" She chuckled as she walked away. Maybe I helped her lighten up and feel more at ease.

As my plate of food sits in front of me steaming, I give it a minute to cool down some. I look around to see if Amanda is anywhere that I can see, and again as I scan by the neighbor's table our eyes come together as if she hasn't taken hers off me. I don't know if it's the alcohol, but she looks better and better every time I look at her. By the end of dinner with another drink or two, she may really be smoking, and not cigarettes if you know what I mean.

My food has cooled off enough that I am ready to dig in and see what this chimichanga is all about. Bite after bite it gets better with each one. I decide I had better come up for air and as I do

Molly comes over and asks how my meal is. I give her a thumbs up as I swallow; then I follow it up with a verbal approval that put a smile on her face. I wash it down with a gulp of my drink and I can't help but notice the smoking neighbor lady's eyes are glued on me as her mouth is engaged in conversation with the man she shares her table with.

Because I really don't know if they are married, I turn my attention fixed in on her hands. They are folded in front of her. They occasionally part as her right hand picks up her glass for a sip. I can't tell looking from here so I focus back on my dinner. It doesn't matter whether they are married or not. They are together and I really would like to meet up with Amanda later, end of story.

Just then, as if it were on cue, my phone beeps. It's a text from Kayla. It reads, "how was your dinner? I am just getting out of work." I answer "I am almost done. My dinner is good. I am at a hotel restaurant." I decided to stop there and not disclose anymore information because I might blow my location. Not that it would be the end of the world, but a plan is a plan. And, one man's Rebel Reprieve is his business. And not to sound bitter, but she went to California to better herself. I am just here to find myself. That's the Jack Daniels taking over my brain.

I wash down some rice with my drink and tip it up as the ice clangs toward my lips. I hold up my glass to Molly and point to it as a standard sign that I will have another. My third drink will be my last here.

I put my phone back in my pocket. I probably don't need it this weekend. I eat the last of my meal and take a few more bites of my salad. Molly shows up with another old Number 7. I thank her as I hold it up as if to toast my neighbor who still looks my way. That's it. When I'm done here I'm going to walk by her to see her ring finger. Then I am going to go out and see if Amanda is still planning on going out when she is done work. Maybe just maybe we can meet up somewhere.

I take the last couple bits of salad and put my fork down and push the plate away as if to surrender. With a wave of my napkin I wipe the corners of my mouth. The girl who delivered my meal came by to bus my table. She smiled and asked "how was your meal?"

"Very good", I replied. I sat back with a huge sigh, sipped my drink and noticed my neighbors are now eating their dinner so I just scan the dining room taking it all in.

The next time Molly comes by I'm going to ask her for my check. The room is somewhat dark, but I can see just fine. I don't know how somebody can see the menu with it so dull. I don't remember it being this dark in here when I ordered, and then it hit me. That was before I had three drinks. Just as I solved that mystery Molly walked by. I asked her for the check.

"Sure thing", she replied. "Let me deliver this and I will get it for you."

So as I waited I check out the neighbor lady and they are engaging in their meals, not each other. I don't believe she has anything on her left ring finger, but I'll see about that soon enough.

Molly arrives with a smile and my check that has a smiley face next to the amount. As I study the check, I spent more on the three drinks than I did on my meal. The amount, including tax, is thirty-six dollars and change. I put on my thinking cap and say, okay, ten percent of thirty six is $3.60; twenty percent is $7.20. I didn't forget Molly waited for me to finish my conversation with Amanda, and her service was excellent. I am not afraid to tip well when I think it is deserving.

I put my card out and as soon as I put it down Molly swept it up and said, "I'll be right back." Again, that's good service. She returned quickly and said, "thanks for coming. Enjoy the rest of your weekend."

"Thank you", I replied. I write down $10.00 for the tip which is close to thirty percent. Forty-six dollars for one person I think to myself. Thanks God I'm alone. I again check out my neighbor lady and they appear to have come to a halt on their food. They are actually talking again. I signed the receipt and took my copy. Since I can't read lips, I will study their body language. It appears they are talking about their meals as their eyes go from each other to the table and back, and little hand movements are dead giveaways.

Then it appears the gentleman neighbor is heading for the men's room. I see this as a good time to excuse myself and head for the exit. As I get up, push my chair in, I walk right past their table. She watched me the whole time come toward her. I nodded as we had eye contact. We both smile and, of course, she had both hands on the table, and there was no ring on her left finger.

As I walk past her, I say "good evening." She answered with a friendly "hello" and I kept walking toward the exit as if I were marching in cadence, after all, my next order of business was to see if Amanda still had plans to go out. That's where my focus was. Neighbor lady was with somebody regardless of whether there were rings involved or not. Amanda, on the other hand, is very much single. That's where I am going to focus.

I walk to the entrance of the restaurant where Amanda was standing, looking at a seating chart or something. She looked up and her beautiful face had this smile that could have meant a thousand things and she said "well, how was your meal?"

I answered "It was very good, as you told me it would be. And the service was good as well", I added. I knew I needed to keep the conversation going, so I said, "Now I just need to figure out what I'm going to do next." I looked at my watch and it was only 7:30 P.M. "What time do you get out of work?" I ask.

She said "I'm usually out at 9:30 P.M."

"Are you still planning on going out with your friend?", I ask.

"She said she would text me before I got out", Amanda replied.

"Oh", I answered. As this moment has become kind of awkward, I say "I'm going to go to my room for awhile. Do you mind if I come back later and see you. I would at least like to buy you a drink when you get out."

Amanda said, "that would be nice."

That answer was just what I had hoped for. She said it with such sincerity I couldn't help but smile as I turned around and stepped toward the lobby. I said, "I'll come back in a while then."

I went down the small flight of stairs, took a right and before I know it I'm at my door. I enter my room and check my watch again and ask myself, what am I going to do for two hours. It's 4:30 P.M. in California so I don't want to call Kayla. Instead I texted her that I'm finished with dinner.

I decide to prepare my clothes for tomorrow. I lay them out on a chair, jacket and ski pants. Then on top of that my sweater and sweat pants, and on top of those my base layer consisting of long johns and long sleeve Under Armour top for warmth. That should be fine as the temperature is supposed to be upper 20's around 9:00 A.M., warming to 32 to 33 degrees.

I then receive a text back. It reads "hope you had a nice dinner. I hope your weekend is everything you want it to be. I'm going out for drinks with a couple of girls from the office. Have a good night, Jake. I'll talk with you later. I love you!" I simply respond "I love you too!! Have fun yourself".

# Chapter Ten

Now I have time to kill. I know I may not hear from Kayla again tonight, and that's a good thing if I do end up going out with Amanda. This is where having a friend to be with would help because I'm not sure what I should do for two hours. I can't drink anymore. So I turn on the television to NBC. The Wheel of Fortune is in the middle of a puzzle. Being one of my favorite game shows, I have to solve this one. The subject is people. They already have the "s", the t's, m's and e's. It's three words. I say "c", like they can hear me, and the woman says "r." The next lady spins the wheel. I say "c" again. She says "d." No "d." Next is a man and he hollers "p", and there's no "p." Okay people, I don't know what the puzzle is, but try a freaking "c." Next lady says "h" and there was one. She spins and says "g." Yes, now we are getting somewhere. She spins again and says "w", bingo.

As we study the incomplete puzzle, she spins. As I have it figured out and she confidently shouts "can I have an "n." Pat announces there are two "n's." Vannah turns them. She says she would like to solve it. "Game show contestant", I holler out just before she repeats after me. "Game show contestant", she hollers as Vannah spins the rest of the letters. Huh, there's the "c" I was looking for while they were getting buzzed out on letters that weren't there.

Buzzed out! I thought I'm going to lose my buzz if I don't drink for these two hours. If I get to have a drink with Amanda that will be a fair trade I thought. The show went to a commercial and I said "oh." I unpacked my gloves, helmet and goggles and placed them on my jacket. I then placed the middle and base layer back into place. Okay. I'm ready. All I need is a ticket. I'll be carving s's all weekend. My heart starts to race with anticipation.

I then sit back down to watch the rest of Wheel of Fortune. I know it's easy to play sitting at home. I have won so much money on this show and have nothing to show for it. I joke to myself, maybe some day I can go to California to visit Kayla and be on the show. Then I can make an ass out of myself in front of millions of people. Or maybe I can just visit Kayla and leave the Wheel on the untouched portion of my bucket list. After all, it's better to be thought of as a fool than to open your mouth and remove all doubt.

Sitting on the edge of my bed I surf the tv looking for something, anything that is going to make the next 90 minutes go by faster. I get Lifetime, I think not, TNT, nah. TBS, oh my God, I totally forgot Atlanta was playing the Celtics in Boston and it's on TBS. I doubt they even have that channel up here. I don't have a clue who plays for Atlanta right now. But I am a Bostonian and my blood pumps with adrenaline when one of the Fab 4 are on. I look at the channel card and sure as shit it's on here. Oh well, who cares if the announcers are biased. It's in Boston and the score is close. Now 9:30 P.M. isn't so far away and it's only the end of the first quarter. The game won't end until around 10:00 P.M. I'll watch as much as I can, but I can't be late. I promised Amanda I'd be there. Okay, the promise was to myself.

Now as the second quarter wears on, I'm feeling my stomach start to churn and growl. It's not a hungry growl though, it's more like a clash of foods that weren't aware the other would be there. After about five minutes of that, I'm starting to feel the need to be super close to a bathroom. Suddenly, my love for the game is interrupted because of that need for the bathroom. So rather than risk it, I get up from my front row seat and head into the bathroom. I turned up the volume a little so I could hear the game, but the sound from the game was silenced by the sound of my bagel, pizza and my dinner being evicted all in about twenty seconds. And to top it off, I hear the pretty neighbor lady and her man friend are now back from the restaurant.

Now I know from experience that these walls are kind of thin, so I hope I am done here. As I complete the paper work, I hear them laughing even over the volume of the game, which now I have turned back down. I reclaimed my front row seat and get back into the game.

As halftime is approaching, it dawns on me I'm going to have to shower before meeting Amanda. I can't go out with a woman of her caliber knowing I'll smell down there. I don't think she's the type that would sleep with a guy on a first date, but I'm not taking any chances, so at halftime I'll take a shower. Honestly, I don't want to sleep with her on the first date. Second date, maybe. I just think she's the type you could bring home to mom and be proud to introduce her.

So, if tonight goes well, and we end it with nothing more than a kiss, then tomorrow can be our real first date as she said she works until 4:00 P.M. and doesn't have to work at the restaurant.

I'll ask her out tomorrow night. Maybe a little dinner and some dancing. I'll figure all that out tonight by just talking and getting to know her as much as possible. All this day dreaming and I hardly noticed the buzzer ending the second quarter of the game. The score is tied at 48. I head to the bathroom, turn on the shower and take off my clothes.

As I get into the shower I start to wonder what I will say as I greet her. What do I say? I know I'm just going to go with the moment. If I rehearse, I don't know if she'll still be at the front desk greeting customers or kitchen or wherever. So I'm going to let the moment present itself and say what seems appropriate. I'm not fake, I'm Jake, and I want to come across as me, not someone I don't even know myself. That would be wrong. So as I rinse off that's my decision. I wash my hair, rinse and I am done. Now I have a plan. All I have to do is get dressed and watch the third quarter. Also, when should I meet up with her, a little before or after 9:30 P.M.? Before will make me seem desperate and anxious; later will make me seem cocky and inconsiderate. Being on time will show I am punctual and a man of my word. Okay, no brainer, 9:30 P.M is it.

As I dry off and exit the bathroom I hear the moans of the pretty neighbor lady. I guess they decided to pass on dessert at the restaurant and have it when they got back to their room. Before I turn the volume back up I silence it completely to listen to just how satisfied or vocal she can get. Who needs porn with neighbors like these.

I watch the third quarter while listening to the sounds of their lovemaking. It seems to me that they aren't a couple who knows what each other likes as she is barking commands like a drill sergeant leading her platoon while they are blindfolded. It may not be right listening, but it's hot. I haven't had this much action in a while and I'm not even a participant.

As she cheers him on he obviously finds the right spot. As she approves with multiple "yeses", he couldn't be any more right. Finally, he voices his approval at the same time she does and just like that it's over. The silence triggers me to turn up the volume as the game is still close. And sure enough, I hear their door shut. I bet she needs a cigarette. That to me is again a turnoff. Really? Lay there a cuddle a bit. Nope, she must have jumped up, put some clothes on and gone out for a smoke. I'm not chasing her this time. I'm lucky I didn't lock myself out the first time.

As I watch the game I slink back into the chair, into almost a reclining position. I'm really looking forward to meeting up with Amanda and her friend. It wouldn't break my heart if her friend didn't show. Then I would have Amanda all to myself, and it would feel more like a date.

As I watch the game, it grows more intense as both teams trade baskets against fierce defensive pressure. That's not something you see in the NBA much, but with two playoff contenders with winning records, I guess it's to be expected. After all, that's how you win games.

As the third quarter draws to a close in this dual of evenly matched teams, I check the time. It's 9:25 P.M. I hate to leave a game like this, but there's a pretty girl that I can't wait to lay my eyes on again. She's about to get off working a double-duty shift and I bet she can't wait to get out of here.

I shut off the tv, straighten my clothes in the mirror, spray on a little cologne on my neck and shirt. I take inventory of my wallet, car keys and room key. I put my jacket over my arm as I shut off the light, close the door and head out to meet my queen. With complete confidence I make my way through the lobby to the entrance of the restaurant. At the podium where I expected to find Amanda, there was nobody. I waited a minute to see if she emerged from the kitchen, but the first person to exit was Molly. I said "Excuse me, Molly, have you seen Amanda?" Molly replied, "I heard she had to leave. Something about her brother being involved in an accident." "Oh", I said dejected as all hell. "I hope he's okay", I said as she continued out into the restaurant. I stood there for a few seconds trying to process this. Did she really get a call? Was her brother really in an accident, or was this her way of blowing me off? Either way, I couldn't help but walk out of there feeling like I just witnessed my best friend sink out of sight in a pool of quicksand.

My hopes of an incredible evening were dashed away from one sentence. As I made my way past my neighbor's door, I heard laughter from the woman who smokes like a chimney. I figure she must smoke alot as the rasp sounds so unattractive, yet her happiness feels like my nose is being rubbed in an ashtray.

I pulled out my room key card and opened my door when the green light gave me the cue. I threw my coat on the chair, grabbed the remote and put the game back on knowing I can at least see the game play out. With any luck the Celtics will pull out a win.

I propped up the pillows to elevate my head so I can lay down and finish the game. I can't help but feel played. As I watch the game with so much less enthusiasm, I realize that I am on a Rebel Reprieve. I came here to escape the city and the life I had as I knew it. Bam! A light goes off! I only booked for two nights. I quickly grab the phone and push zero. A male voice picked up and said "front desk."

"Hi, my name is Jake Christopher in Room 103. I lucked into this room off a cancellation and booked it for two nights. Can you tell me how long the people who canceled had it for?", I ask.

"Through Wednesday night, leaving on Thursday", he replied.

"Has anyone booked it Sunday through Wednesday night", I ask. "No? Well I have decided to stay through Wednesday. I would like to book it through Wednesday. Can you put it on the card I paid with? It should be on file."

"Yes, it can be added, but I need you to come to the office at some point and sign", the front desk person said.

"Okay. I'll be there shortly. I want to see the end of this game", I said. As quickly as my hopes were dashed by Amanda, I realized that I am here to ski and I can't dwell on things I have no control over. I learned that when my dad died; when Kayla left for California; and when I lost my job.

It's time to be a little selfish and remind myself that I made a conscious decision to do this and that's why I said nothing to anyone. I came to enjoy myself and figure out what I want. Screw Kayla, and screw Amanda. I don't like to be played. Right now I'm going to go to the office, sign for the extra nights and call it a night.

As the clock winds down, it's not looking good. It appears the Celtics are on the losing end of this home game. The Hawks and their few fans in the crowd, not to mention the biased commentators, have it in hand.

I grabbed my room key, wallet and went up to the front desk and took care of my room through Wednesday. Now it's nothing but me and my skis and hopefully mother nature as she is supposed to dump some fresh powder Sunday night into Monday.

I have nothing to worry about for days. My neighbors have quieted as I glide by their door to turn in for the evening and call it a night. I guess I'll go to bed and be thankful I won't wake up with a hangover in the morning, not that I was planning on getting ripped, but I never did in the past. My last thoughts are, as I shut off the light, before I head out in the morning I'll call Ann and tell her I'm fine and hopefully I'll get to say hi to my nephew, Jack. Just thinking of that little boy calms me and gives me peace. He is so young and carefree. He is inquisitive and his love for life makes me want to be a kid again. These are thoughts that I needed to relax and fall asleep. No need to set the alarm, I'll wake up when I wake up.

# Chapter Eleven

My eyes pop open. I glance at the clock and it's 6:30 A.M. Twenty-four hours after the fact, this plan is coming together. I want to lay here and stay under the covers, but I really have to pee. So I bound out of bed and go to alleviate my erection. Since I taste the cotton in my mouth, I quickly brush my teeth to get rid of that nonsense.

I climb back under the covers and look at my phone. God, I wish I had Amanda's number. I would text her to see how her brother is. I really want to believe that story because she seems so incredible. As my mind quickly switches gears, I think I'd better call Anne.

"Hello, sis, how are you?", I asked.

She replies, "I'm fine, the question is, how are you, and where are you?"

I quickly replied "I'm fine. I'm a little dejected because I don't know if I got stood up last night, or if the girl's brother really had an accident."

"Oh, dear! Is that what she told you?", Anne asked.

"No. I went to the restaurant when she got off work and she wasn't there. When I asked for her, they said she had to leave because her brother had an accident", I told her.

"Oh. Do you think it's the truth?, she asked.

"I don't know what to think right now. It's pretty much how my luck has gone. Hey, is Jack up? I'd like to talk to my favorite nephew."

"No", she replied, "he's still fast asleep. He usually wakes up between 7:00 and 7:30."

"Wake him up", I said.

"No, I don't dare to", she chuckled.

"Why?, I asked.

"Because he's a bear if I wake him up early. He's in hibernation and I just let him get up when he gets up. It's better that way. Plus, it's Saturday", she said.

"Oh, yeah", I said. "I kind of forgot. Hopefully I didn't wake you up."

"No", she said, "I was awake."

"Okay, good. All right. I'll call tomorrow for sure, I promise. I'm here through Wednesday. Love you, bye", I said. I quickly hung up as I purposely skirted that she asked where I was. I don't want anyone to know.

Am I being selfish or am I sticking to my guns that this is as I've labeled it, my Rebel Reprieve? I'm going with Rebel Reprieve.

Nobody has cut me any slack since my life has gone downhill from the time dad died. Downhill, I thought as I glance at my skis. Suddenly I felt a sparkle in my eye. At that moment I pull back the curtain and it's starting to get light outside. The mountain doesn't open for nearly an hour and a half. What do I do? I sat back down on my bed, grabbed the remote and put the television on. I pushed 3 for CBS hoping for a local news station for the weather. Bingo, CBS out of Burlington and it's showing the weather. The anchor is a lanky looking man who looks more like a high school Biology teacher or something, with gray hair and glasses.

He shows the weather system that's moving in tomorrow night. Sure enough, it's going to snow! I'm so glad I booked it for a few more days. Today looks good, high of 30 degrees, sun and clouds; tomorrow is mostly cloudy with snow moving in in the evening. I'm sure I'll be like a kid on Christmas Eve tomorrow night!

With any luck Amanda will come looking for me after the thing with her brother is resolved. That is if he's all right. I sure hope so. It will all work out if what I was told happened, and she is back to work on schedule at 8:00 A.M. I'll definitely see her in the lobby in a little while before I go out to meet the shuttle.

As I lay on my bed and watch the news, it seems quite refreshing to me that the "news" is mostly stories of happy things, or at least not story after story of gang-related crimes, or people hit by cars and the driver sped away. These are actual feel-good things that don't make the news broadcasts in Boston because they aren't tragic. Rarely do they show an inspirational story that actually hits you in the "feels" as they say. You know what? I'm going to throw some clothes on and go to the lobby and get a coffee and pastry or something to eat that will hold me over.

On my way out the door I grab my room key and make my way up the small set of stairs and immediately the aroma of coffee draws me in that direction. As I wait my turn I spy the registration desk and there's no sign of Amanda. I don't know why I'm bummed. It's only 7:15 A.M.

As I pour my coffee and eye my pastry, I complete this mission by grabbing both and heading back to the hallway that quickly takes me to my room. In order to pull this off and not have an accident in the hallway, I set my coffee down, insert the key card, pull it up and voila! I'm in. I get in the room, set down my key card, coffee and pastry on the table. I go back to close the door gently so as to not break the quiet and wake the neighbors. And there it is, she starts moaning, and it gets louder and louder. She must know how much noise she makes. Unless, of course, she's hard of hearing. That I don't believe.

I pull up a chair to the table in front of my coffee and sit down to enjoy my little breakfast and audio show. God, I envy that guy as he's really starting to put it to her. Now I hear them both as they moan in harmony to the sound of their bodies slamming together. I envision what position they are sharing in this moment. As I listen to her intently, I envision I was the one pounding her doggy-style, pulling her hair back like the reins of a stallion fully in gallop and ready to unleash. She must be an exhibitionist because she screams and giggles all in pleasure and it's like she wants to be heard. "Harder!", she screams, almost out of breath. "Harder, harder!" I can definitely feel I'm getting harder as I grab myself totally forgetting about my coffee and pastry. As they go for broke I find myself stroking as the adrenaline pumps through my body. I hope they can hold out as I have only just begun, but as she screams through the wall I picture her pretty face and spectacular body and know between the excitement, lack of sex and the speed with which I thrust, this threesome is bound to finish together.

"Give it to me", she screams, "harder, harder, give it to me. I'm going to cum, I'm going to cum. Cum with me", as the bed slams against the wall and my hand works quickly as if there was no border between us. I envision exploding all over her back, as I draw near to climax, and at the same time she lets out this relentless "Oh my God, yes, yes, yes." He moans a few satisfying grunts at the same time and says "take that baby, take that", as we all release simultaneously. Mine was I envisioned all over her naked body, laying face down away from me as it drips down the small of her back. As she lay there loving every drop of my semen hugging her skin, I continue to ride on her ass as to squeeze every drop out of my throbbing muscle into the napkin I used to carry my pastry.

Wow, I thought as silence now bestows the barrier that once seemed like it wasn't there. After several seconds, I hear her giggle like a little girl who just got on a quarter horsey ride at the department store front. I sat there for a minute as I felt such a release and a satisfaction like I never felt from masturbating before. I guess because I had never done it to a live encounter, or where I felt very much apart of the exhibition. She is pretty awesome. I still don't care that she smokes, but son of a bitch, she sure can fuck.

I roll up the napkin to trap my humongous load within. I take a bite of my pastry and sip my coffee like my intention was when I came back to my room. My heart is still racing as I have no idea what they may be doing. I do know that I haven't heard her door shut, meaning it's time for a cigarette.

I glance at the time and realize the shuttle shows up at 8:00 A.M. My mind quickly prompts me to jump up and start getting dressed. If I get up there early I'll have time to see Amanda and ask her how her brother is and maybe make some dinner arrangement for tonight since she's out at 4:00 P.M. and doesn't have to work in the restaurant.

I get all of my clothes on, finish my coffee and pastry and grab my skis and pause. I ask myself, do I have everything? I do a quick inventory of my clothing, right down to or up to my helmet and goggles. Skis, boots, poles, check. I grab some cash for my ticket and food and leave my wallet - I don't need the bulk. I can buy a water from the cooler in the lobby.

I slide a room key and cash in my ski pants pocket, zip it up and look back in my room disgusted I didn't even make my bed. The rolled up napkin on my table. Gross, I think and chuckle as I flip the Do Not Disturb sign on my door handle. I'll take care of that when I get back. I've convinced myself that I'm here for me, who cares what anyone else thinks. They won't attempt to clean my room with the sign up.

I ramble loudly in my ski boots up the stairs with my skis and poles and walk calmly and recklessly toward the cooler. I set my stuff down and grab a water and saunter over to the registration desk to pay and there's no sign of Amanda. I ask the young lady at the desk as I dig out my money if she's seen Amanda.

As she takes my money she replies "I'm sorry. I'm new here. I don't know who Amanda is yet. I just started last week", she added.

"Okay", I said, "I thought she started at 8:00 A.M.."
"Well, it's a few minutes til", she said.

Just then the shuttle driver walked in and said "if anyone is ready go to, I've got to take off early for the first ride. My boss needs my help ASAP, so I've got to go."

I said "I'm ready", so I grabbed my skis and poles and headed out the door. A couple also in the lobby boarded the minibus with me. All the while I'm glancing for any sign of Amanda.

# Chapter Twelve

As we pulled out onto the road and headed up the Access Road, I don't know what to think. Is it worse than I had hoped? Was Amanda's brother hurt bad, or is she totally blowing me off? It's hard telling, but based on my luck these last couple of months, I'm picturing a Dear John letter. I'm trying to be positive though. If there's one thing I've learned, it's life isn't always as it seems.

I'll ski all day. After all, I'm going to be one of the first people in line. I'll meet some folks and I'll grab the shuttle early enough to get back to the hotel before 4:00 P.M. when Amanda said she gets done work. She has the night off and tomorrow also, so that is the perfect plan that gives me hope and calms me down. The shuttle driver pulls up in the unloading zone at the gondola. The three of us get off and there's already a handful of people in line. We unload our skis, walk up to the ticket window then wait to board.

This is awesome! I'm on the first gondola to the top. The first run is going to cleanse so much of the bull shit that has happened for the last few months. I feel like a kid again, just filled with excitement and I know my life has got to turn around. The cars are filing into the parking lot in a slow moving convoy as each one passes by in envy of those of us waiting for the signal. At that moment the attendant says it's time to load up. Up, up and away, I think to myself. As I look back at the parking bays, they are already filling the second bay, and it's only 8:15 A.M. I marvel at the beauty of the view all the way up and can't wait to hear the click, click as I step into my bindings.

Finally we get to the top even though it only took like seven minutes. I was ready to get this party started. As I get out and grab my skis I have to pee. I have two choices and since I'm a guy, I'm not going to let the opportunity slip to be one of the first to make some turns. I'll just take a leak off the side of the trail. I lay out my skis, poles in hand and step in. I pull my goggles down off my helmet and put them over my eyes. I ready my poles and head over off the back side, seemingly away from my fellow passengers as they discuss their journey down. I'm all alone as I carve my way down this fresh virgin-groomed trail. This is heavenly I think to myself. As with every turn my troubles are further in the past. This is therapy in motion. The view is to die for. I can see in a southwesterly direction as I fall in toward the backside of Bear Mountain. I'm not sure I've skied this trail before as I feel the need to pee becoming an unbearable condition.

I decide to ski off trail so that nobody comes up behind me and catches me mid-stream. Into the woods, out of sight, out of mind, carving through trees like a slalom skier going for time. Finally I stop and unzip my ski pants. Like a kid who held it too long I frantically extract and spray like a fireman just trying to control his hose.

Awww, what a relief! There's no way I was going to get caught in here. Awww, the mission is accomplished! As I get myself squared away, now it's time to carve my way back onto the trail. I am gliding down, seemingly back on track. Along the side of the mountain, turn after turn it's getting thicker and steeper. "I know the trail is over here somewhere", I tell myself as I carve through trees and rocks. All of a sudden I felt myself fall with nothing underneath me. In the blink of an eye my body is airborne. Crash!!! Ahhhh!!! As my body stopped suddenly my skis detach, my left leg is twisted underneath me and all of a sudden the most intense pain I've ever felt in my life screamed from my left knee. I locked my lips together trying to hold it in, but I couldn't. I let out the most horrifying scream that must have been heard for miles.

I look around but can't see anything because the snow is imbedded in my goggles. I raise them and look up to see that I fell about fifteen feet and landed on a ledge. I screamed in pain again. My knee is fucking killing me. I realize at this point I really don't hurt anywhere else. I try to stand up and the pain is excruciating. "No fucking way", I think to myself. What did I do? Thank God I had my helmet on. All I can think about is my knee and how excruciating the pain is.

I grab one of my poles and try to stand. "Jesus", I say. Even if I get up, what am I dong to do? I can't climb up so I crawl over to the edge and look down. "What the fuck?", I say as I look down over and its ledgy snow-covered rocks for quite a ways. Spruce trees are growing out of the side of the mountain. I look back at the ledge behind me and there is a cave-looking hole that I can't really see into.

I remember my phone. I hope I didn't break it in the fall. I pull it out of my jacket and look at it. It looks okay. Good. Who do I call, nobody knows I'm here. I'll call Anne. She was my last call. I press recall. What do you mean no service area? I'm on top of a friggin' mountain. I'll try Basin Ski Shop. No service again. How could that fucking be? No bars! I try 911 and still it wont go through. I decide to try to text Anne. Unable to send!

What the fuck? I look around again. I pull out my water and take a sip. All of a sudden it becomes clear. I'm stranded. I have no service and nobody has a fucking clue where I am. My knee is twisted and is so painfully tight I cant stand, much less walk or climb.

I drag myself across this little ledge that may be twelve feet and grab my skis and go back to the edge and stand them on the edge in the snow, crossed facing out so the colors can be seen. Who the fuck is going to see them? Nobody knows I'm here and I can't see anything but the other side of the ravine. I must be in a pocket where my phone isn't picking up a signal.

"This isn't good", I think to myself. What am I supposed to do? What did I do to my knee? So many emotions right now. I can't even think straight. I have no way to build, much less start a fire. All I have is a bottle of water. My phone is useless. It's early in the day, and I now am starting to think my Rebel Reprieve is going to kill me.

I look over at the cave. That's my cover if I need it. I'd better check it out. So I drag myself across the ledge with a ski pole at my side. I inch my way into the darkness and see it goes in a ways. I grab my phone out of my pocket and get my arms out in front of me, which isn't easy because it's so cramped. It might be three feet high. I turn on my phone screen and see nothing but black for about ten feet in. I fumble with my phone and turn on the flashlight. As I look back into the cave I still see black, but it looks like fur. I go right to left and holy shit, it's a bear! "It's a fucking bear", I think to myself. It's head is tucked under its front leg toward me, and it's not moving. It's asleep I think, and then I realize it's hibernating you fucking dumb ass. I'm stuck on a ledge. Nobody knows I'm here, and there's a hibernating bear in my only source of shelter.

Fuck my life. This trip just turned into the end of my life. Slowly I carefully slide back out onto the ledge. I've got to keep my head together so I can think. God I wish I could Google hibernating bears. But no, I have a phone that's useless to me. If he's hibernating, what will it take to wake him up? If he wakes up, will he eat me? God dammit! I can't make any noise. I don't dare cry, even though I want to. What do I do? I'm going to die if he wakes up. What do I do? Fuck it. If he does wake up, I want to already be dead. I can't handle the thought of being eaten alive. So I've decided before my phone charge dies, and I die, I'm going to record this so if anyone finds my body, if there's anything left, or they find my phone, they will know what happened to me.

I point the camera to me. There, record. "To my family and friends. I, Jake Christopher, on this day, January 30, 2017, while skiing on what was supposed to be the first day of the rest of my life, I find that it could very well be the last days of my life. I love you all very much and it wasn't supposed to be like this. While skiing out of bounds to pee I skied off this ledge and royally fucked up my knee. I couldn't get myself out and I have no service to summon help. I am stuck, and to make matters worse, I have no supplies and have found that I am not alone. Inside this cave is a hibernating bear."

"If there is no sign of me, but my phone is found, I was most likely eaten by the bear, or I am further down the mountain below the steep ledge because I desperately tried something. Either way, I want you all to know how sorry I am for being selfish, and I now know how important it is for someone to know where a person is."

"Anne, you and Jack are my only family and I want you to know how much I love you. I'm sorry I purposely didn't tell you where I was, I see now how selfish this decision was."

"Jack, I want you to grow up into a man with honor and integrity. I was looking forward to teaching you how to play sports and watching you grow on the fields and basketball court. You were the son I never got a chance to have, and I will miss you very much." With tears welling in my eyes, I know I have to continue. "Take care of your mother. I know you will. When you are old enough to have girlfriends, treat them like gold. Be a gentleman and don't be afraid to show your feelings. If you love a girl enough and can't imagine life without her, hold on to her and ask her to marry you if you know she feels the same way. If you don't, another opportunity may arise for her and before you know it she's gone for good. I love you, Jack, you make me proud."

"Kayla, you were the love of my life. I never wanted to say goodbye to you. After my dad died I realized how short life is and I decided to ask you to marry me. I bought a ring and was going to propose Christmas Eve. But when the job offer happened, I saw how excited you were and couldn't stand in your way of following your dream. I had to let you go. I'm not going to say that I didn't hope it wouldn't work out because I did. But, I wasn't going to be the reason. You will always be my love and I'm sorry you found out this way. I thought you had a right to know what really was in my heart. I hope California makes you happy because you deserve to be happy. Don't have regrets. Everything happens for a reason. I want you to marry and have children. I know you have dreamed about that and someday I hope to be able to watch over you with a smile. I'll say hello to my dad for you. I know how much he adored you, and you him. I'll be happy to see him and I know once he got to heaven his Alzheimer's went away. It will be good to have him back in my life. So don't be sad. I didn't die tragically and it's nobody's fault but my own. I will always love you and I know you will me. If you ever have a boy, I would be honored if you'd name him Jake. Take care of yourself and I pray now more than ever that you succeed. Love always, Jake."

"Amanda, I want to say a few things to you. Although our story never got a chance to be written, you made me feel special in our two brief encounters. First on Friday when I checked in. I couldn't believe how beautiful you were. I got a feeling that I had not encountered in quite some time. I felt alive, yet my nerves held me back. Then that night at the restaurant I felt like I got a second chance, and I wasn't going to let it slip by.

I was devastated to hear about your brother's accident. I truly hope he is okay. When I got to the restaurant to meet you, finding that out I hoped for the best. I have to admit, a part of me felt like I was getting blown off, but I know you are better than that and it wasn't all about me at that point. That was a time when family needs to be together and you were needed. I hoped to see you before I went skiing, but when you weren't there at the front desk I figured you were still with your brother. Just know you made an impression on me, and I wasn't ready to say goodbye to you at that point in my life. In fact, I was looking at it as a new chapter that was destined to be written. Instead maybe God was giving me a look at an angel before he called for me. You are truly an amazing person. I wish you all the happiness, and that your brother is okay."

"To everyone else, friends, cousins, uncles, aunts, co-workers, Mr. Rodgers, I've always tried to be a good person, kind, helpful and honest. If I offended you in any way, please forgive me. Goodbye, I love you all! This is Jake Christopher signing off." He hangs his head as he shut off his phone, tears streaming down his cheeks.

# Chapter Thirteen

I can't believe it. I'm so mad at myself, and my knee is killing me. I need to think. Does anyone know I'm here? I can't believe this. I kept it a secret. My egotistical mind convinced myself that nobody needed to know. I'm going to die out of selfish pity. "Helloooo!!!", I hollered. Nothing. What do I have on me? My phone and a bottle of water. My phone is useless and it's going to die. My water bottle will empty and that will be useless. No matches, no lighter. I'm going to freeze before I starve to death, I guess. And to top it off, I have a bear that is scaring me to death. Fact is, I can't kill it. Even if I could, I can't cut it up or cook it. So if a bear is in hibernation, it must be a deep sleep. Almost comatose-like where I don't think it can wake up until spring. I have this ski pole. Should I crawl back in and poke it? If I do and it wakes up, what do I do? If it doesn't wake up, does that mean it's asleep until spring? Again, I wish I could Google this shit.

How do I survive out in the open on this ledge? I can't do anything for myself out here. What about at night? The temperature will drop and it's supposed to snow tomorrow night. I need the cave, I need the cover, and I need to know that the bear won't bother me, and I won't bother it. As night falls, I know I'm going to have to crawl back in there.

It suddenly dawns on me that I left the Do Not Disturb sign on the door so nobody will go in my room. They'll probably just figure I wanted privacy. Right now I wouldn't care if they found my bed not made and the soiled napkin there, at least they'd figure out after a day or two I wasn't there.

The hours pass slowly and the sun is now on this side of the mountain, but it's going to go down pretty soon and it'll be dark. So many thoughts are going through my head. I'm trying to drink my water sparingly, but I am so thirsty. Not to mention how hungry I am.

It's now getting dark so I had better crawl into the cave. I can't lean against this ledge all night. I'll freeze. At least in the cave I won't feel the wind and the cold so much. Not to mention while I still have the light from my screen, I can look at the bear and kind of figure him out. Will he wake up and eat me, or will he stay asleep.

I drag my half lifeless lower body back inside where it's pitch black. The bear is seemingly in the same position. Thank God he's not snoring! Oh my God, if I snore will it wake him? Maybe I shouldn't sleep. This is exhausting. At least if he wakes up and kills me in my sleep, I won't feel it.

I'm just going to prop myself up against the wall as best I can over here. If only I can get comfortable. My knee is fucked. I have nothing to make a splint. I could use my ski poles but I don't have anything to tie them with. Plus, they are my only defense. Like I'm going to fight off a bear with them I joke sarcastically to myself.

I'm just going to flip on my light every now and then and check on the bear. Or, if I hear him move, moan or stir in any way, I'll shine the light on him so if he sees it, maybe it will scare him and he'll bolt across my legs and out the cave. That would be awesome, except he'll probably do more damage which will hurt like a mother fucker. I've looked at every scenario I can imagine and given the circumstances, in the end of all of them, I'm going to die. It is only a matter of how I will die that I'm not even going to get to choose.

I'm going to huddle up as best I can and try to stay warm. I wish I had my Sox cap. I'd rather be found in that than have this helmet strapped to my scull. At least he won't be able to eat my head, I chuckle. I'll close my eyes and try to imagine peace and warmth. Strangely enough, I am feeling at peace. I'm not accepting I'm going to die, I just feel peace all of a sudden. I'm still chilly, but at least my gloves are well insulated, as well as my under layers. Eventually though, I'm sure the cold will overpower me as the temperature is supposed to drop.

As crazy as this sounds, I was able to fall asleep. In fact, the last time I looked at my watch it was 8:00 P.M. It's now 5:30 A.M. and I'm alive! I am cold, my leg feels like it weighs a thousand pounds, but I'm alive! My phone has about a 10% charge left, which I'm only going to use to check on the bear. He hasn't moved. It's almost like he's dead, but I can see his very shallow compressions from his comatose breathing. Boy, do I envy that. As I lay here it dawns on me that when I spoke with Anne yesterday morning and asked for Jack, she said he was still sleeping and wouldn't wake him up because he sleeps like a bear. I'm going to call the bear "Jack".

It's like an instant connection. Jack, I said, can you hear me? As I hold the light at his face, nothing. Not a reaction to be had. Can I talk to you, Jack? Can I call you Jack? Are you even a male bear? You're so curled up I can't see if you're a male or a female. I'm going to assume you are a male. That would make you a boar. Well, hopefully you bore me, but not to death, I joke.

So Jack, do you come here often? Is this your cave? Do you have a girlfriend? I bet you have several. You're probably a stud, that's why you sleep so well. I wish you could tell me when you will wake up. Maybe I don't want to know. Looks like I'll probably be dead by then though, so it won't matter.

Can you promise me something though, Jack? Promise me when you wake up you won't eat me. Can you promise me that? Will you shake on it? As I said that, without thinking, I reached out and touched his paw. He didn't move. Jack? I said, do you feel that? Do you feel anything?

I decided to get more brave and see just what I can do. I took my ski pole and I poked him gently, nothing. I poked him a little harder and nothing still. I grabbed his paw and lifted his leg and let it back down. He is lifeless.

I waited a few seconds and picked up his paw again. This time I reached out with my other hand and felt his claws. Oh yeah, he has some very large claws. I quickly put his leg back down. I waited a few minutes and he hasn't had any kind of reaction. I took my gloves off, and this time I picked up his paw and stuck my hand under his leg. I felt how warm it was. Not only did I feel the warmth under his so-called armpit, but I felt the warmth coming off his body. He actually is giving off heat, I thought.

Damn, I thought. I took the last swallow from my water bottle. I dragged myself out onto the ledge and started to pack snow into the water bottle filling it up. It's now 8:00 A.M., it's light out, and fairly chilly. I slide back into the cave and over to Jack. I pick up his paw, slide the water bottle under his leg, tuck it under his armpit and lay his leg back down. I then backed away to where I slept last night and waited. As I had hoped, Jack is cooperating. He hasn't moved a muscle. The icy water bottle doesn't bother him.

After waiting an hour, I slide back over to his lifeless body and lift up his leg and grab the water bottle. I hold up my dying phone to the bottle and as I had hoped, the snow is now almost water. I have water and with all the snow on the ledge, I will have all that I need. Plus, it supposed to snow tonight. Hopefully not as much as I had hoped before since I'm not skiing powder any time soon.

It's frightening to think, will I ever ski again? I feel like I tore everything in my knee. Even though it's squished in my thermals, I can feel it. It is swollen to probably twice its size. It scares me to think about that, but given my situation, I'm going to die with this busted knee anyway.

As soon as the sun peeks into the cave, I decided to crawl out onto the ledge and assess the situation. I know I'm on the southwest side facing inward towards the other side of the ravine. I can't see out toward the west or anything, but I'm in the open enough where I can see that it's maybe 300 to 400 feet to the other side.

It's supposed to be thirty degrees today. If I stay in the sun as long as I can, I won't be too cold, and maybe I can pack snow around my knee to help with the swelling. I prop myself up and cover my left leg in the snow. I wish I had something on my feet other than ski boots. Thank God I have some good ones that have kept my feet pretty warm so far. My feet are just so cramped and uncomfortable. It's not going to harm me if I unbuckle my boots. In fact, maybe I can pull them off to let my feet breathe and wiggle my toes. I've had my boots on for about twenty-six hours now.

I slide my right foot out of its boot and wiggle my toes. That feels really good. I lean down to unbuckle my left boot and I can barely reach my foot. My leg won't bend, and as hard as it is to reach it, I realize I'm never going to be able to reach down and put that boot back on. If I take it off, I may never get it back on, so I have no choice but to leave it on. I'm so sorry left foot, I can't take the chance. You will suffer frost bite if I can't get it back on.

The sun does feel good, so I pull off my helmet. I slide my goggles off of it and put them on to shield my eyes. I can't believe I didn't bring sunglasses. Not a necessity, but another thing I didn't prepare myself with. I did tell myself during my inventory Friday morning, it's better to have it and not need it, than to need it and not have it. I didn't listen or practice that, now did I?

I stare out at the bottoms of my skis as I take a swig of water. They are just as I had left them, crossing each other as if to say "I'm here!!!" Help me!!!" Too bad nobody knows where I am. I set myself up to die on the side of this mountain.

If only I had thought of it during my goodbye video. I would have suggested spreading some of my ashes here. Just a few since this is where I expired. Maybe a few on the huge rock at the top where you can look out and pretty much see in all directions. Sadly, I have nobody but Anne to do this, and I don't know how humanly possible it is to get ashes to this spot. I know it's barely possible though, haha. I still have my sense of humor, at least for now I do.

I must say that the sun is calming and it's so quiet, except for the hawk that lets out an occasional call. I'm going to close my eyes and whatever happens, happens. The warmth from the sun mixed with the crisp air on my face lulls me into a peaceful time where the only thing that matters is right now.

I'm drifting to a place that feels serene. I can't explain it. My pain is in neutral. The clouds, although occasional, shield the sun with brief increments of relief. As the clouds pass by, the sun peeks back at me with rays that stretch from the heavens to my body. What is happening? I feel so in tune with the sky and this hypnotic force. The rays are the stairway to the Pearly Gates, and beyond the sun is my acceptance to leave and become one with those who have gone before me. I must be dreaming

I see my dad's face, I see his arms. I feel like I'm floating before him. He shakes his head "no" and whispers, "God is not ready for you yet. He is not here with me now. He sent me to offer strength and assurance that there is a place for you here, but you are not ready. You can choose to give up, and he will understand."

I want this feeling to last forever, I thought. Again my dad whispered, "it will be just like it, just not now. Do not be afraid, Jack needs you!" With that he was gone. The clouds formed where he stood and I felt my spirit descend back to the ledge. There was a comforting feeling that overcame my being. I can't explain it, but for what may have been a dream, it seemed like reality. Suddenly I'm not afraid to die. I just have a reason to live. There is no one I could have believed more than my dad.

In that next moment I see Jack playing. He's older. There I am in the stands with Anne as Jack hits a home run. As he rounds the bases, he looks at us and smiles. The feeling matches the feeling I had with my dad. "I want that feeling to last forever", I said. Again I hear my dad's voice say "it will be just like that, always. Jack needs you." "I understand. Boy, do I understand. I love you, dad!", I said. With that I awoke still propped up, my right boot off, left boot unbuckled. My left leg was still covered with snow. My goggles were still in place. Everything was just how it was when I closed my eyes. The only thing that changed was me. I now know that I can't give up. It's not about me. It's about Jack. I gave Jack my word I would always be there for him. Even though nobody knows I'm here, I have to believe. If I don't make it, I have a place with my dad. Either way, I win.

# Chapter Fourteen

I'm going to sit here and finish my water. Hopefully I can pee. Then I'll pack the bottle with snow, go in for the night and put the water bottle back under Jack's arm. I wonder how Amanda is? I wonder how her brother is doing. Will she check on me? As far as she knows, I was checking out today. She has Sundays and Mondays off, so I know I'll never see her again.

I take a deep breath and try to put that out of my head. She really is very nice, and absolutely gorgeous. I don't for a second believe she was out of my league. She was so friendly and as I think back, she was very open to meeting up with me. I bet she thinks now that I blew her off. I never got the chance to get her number or anything. It wouldn't do me any good to have it, but at least I would know where we stood.

I crawled back into the cave after repacking the water bottle with snow, putting on my boot, buckling both, putting my helmet on and goggles back on my helmet. My phone is completely dead, so I shove it in my jacket pocket. Hopefully it's still there when, and if, my body is found.

I place the bottle under Jack's arm. I'm just going to refer to it as his arm, it's just me here. I crawl back to the wall and wait. As the sky darkens, the opening turns black. It's time to settle in. The cold is getting to me as I remove the water bottle and take a sip. I place it next to me and think, you know, Jack hasn't moved a muscle since I got here. I'm well aware that his body is warm. What if I just curl up in front of him to take advantage of the warmth radiating off his body? He's not going anywhere. He's not waking up I'm convinced of that. Jack, can I curl up and kind of spoon you, buddy? Or be spooned by you? That seems more like it. Do you mind? I didn't think so.

You don't mind that I named you after my nephew do you? Jack's a really good kid. You would like him. In fact, he sleeps like a bear. That's why I'm calling you Jack. This might seem kind of boring to you, but talking to you gives me hope. So don't wake up and kill me. You promise? I know I can trust you.

I may just lay here and babble. I'm going to ask you questions that you won't be able to answer. I'm going to tell you things you may not understand. Just understand that I'm lonely and I just need to talk. OMG, I sound like a girl. Bare with me, Jack. LOL, I can't believe I just said that either.

Thank you for having this ledge here, buddy. If it wasn't here, I would have fallen even further into the ravine. Who knows if I would have survived. I would have wrapped myself around trees, broken bones and done a whole lot more damage to my body. Yeah, my knee is messed up. Hopefully its repairable and I'm alive to get the repairs. I'm going to shut up now and hopefully fall asleep. Thank you for letting me cuddle with you. I can feel the warmth from you. Hopefully your sleeping skills rub off on me and we both get a good night's sleep. Good night, Jack. See you in the morning.

As I lay there trying to fall asleep, suddenly a coyote lets out a howl. He's not that far away. Then a few minutes later I hear a bark and that's even closer. I reach for my ski pole just in case. I came out of my spoon position and square myself straight on with my back up against Jack. Sure as shit I hear foot steps pressing in the snow on the ledge. All of a sudden I can see his outline peering into the darkness with which I lay, scared out of my mind, but ready with my pointed tip wishing it were a dagger. He growls a little and takes a step in and "wham" I gave him the tip right in the face. It screamed in pain and was gone instantly. "There, you mother fucking one-eyed son of a bitch", I yelled.

I get ready again, praying that was enough to convince him to search for dinner elsewhere. I sat for hours ready for his return. He never returned. I hope in the morning I find an eyeball skewed against the basket of my pole. I got him good, and maybe it was in the eye.

The next morning after it started getting light, I could see the crack of dawn had broken. I crawled to the entrance with my ski pole ready, just in case. Just as predicted, when I got to Vermont, there was several inches of fresh powder on the ledge. The coyote tracks were barely visible, but I could see where it had been. I had to brush it away from the already vertically challenging entrance. As alone as I felt, I could not believe how beautiful the trees looked on the other side of the ravine. Man, do I wish I was boarding the Gondolas to be the first to carve my way down the trails in this stuff. A skier's paradise, the oasis of every dreamer's dream. Then it hit me. My tracks that led off the trail and to my location are now history. Not that anyone would have ever found them. Now it's just another nail in my coffin.

I take a sip of my water. I'm still grateful at this point. Sure, I'm hungry, but I have water. Sure I'm cold, but I have a good source of heat and I'm not frostbitten. I know I can't drag myself out of here. I can't go down, the back side of Killington is nothing but woods for miles. I am a snail and I wouldn't make it even if I knew which direction to go in. Plus, it's fifteen feet straight up above me. I'm stuck on this rock ledge shelf until God is ready for me, so my dad said.

I'll just hang out on my deck in this brilliant sunshine and make the most of it. Hopefully later it will warm up to where I can pull off my boot and helmet again. I think it would be best to drink the last of this water and refill it with this nice fresh snow, put it under Jack's armpit and have water for today. I can eat the snow as well, but it's not as refreshing as the water. So that's what I'll do.

I lay next to Jack while his body heat provides me water. I can't help but strike up a conversation. You know, Jack, it snowed like six inches over night. The groundhog will hopefully predict six more weeks of winter, and hopefully he's right. You just take your time during these next several weeks and stay relaxed. I'll keep you informed as to how it's going out there.

Do you base your hibernation period on the Ol' Punxsutawney Phil's prediction? He's only a groundhog, or as I like to call him, a "woodchuck", but people sure do make a big fuss over the shadow thing. Let's see, ground hog day is February 2nd and Today is the first, so tomorrow is Ground Hog Day. God I hope he sees his shadow and theres 6 more weeks of winter.

What's the first thing a hibernating bear does when he wakes up? Are you all groggy and punch-drunk where you wander around trying to come out of it, or do you go straight for food? There's no berries yet, and there aren't human bird feeders up here you can rob. You're pretty much a real freaking bear. You live in the mountains and survive on the wilderness. I know that besides berries you eat meat. What's your favorite kind of meat? Black bears aren't notorious for killing humans. We don't taste good anyway. Do you search for dumpsters to raid? Do you know they make bear-proof dumpsters now? They do. I've seen them. That's pretty depressing, isn't it? Search and find a great smelling dumpster and it's bear-proof.

How's my bottle of water doing? Yeah, buddy, it's all melted. Thank you, Jack. You're like a microwave for crying out loud. Sweet dreams. I'm going to hang out on our deck. See you this afternoon as the sun decides to disappear behind the Empire state. Keep the home fires burning. I'll come back with another bottle of snow for you to melt.

As I crawl back outside, I decide I'd better go look at my skis to see if the snow stuck to the other side of them when it fell. No idea who would ever see them from there. If they did they'd be more lost than I am. But, hey, you never know. I can't rule anything out. My life depends on it.

My skis look fine. Once again I push my skis back down into the snow so they are crossed. I crawl back over to my spot and grab my ski pole to keep by my side just in case that son of a bitching coyote comes back. Thank God it was just one. When they pack up to hunt, they are far more brave and far more vicious. I don't think I would have fared so well had there been a pack of them.

# Chapter Fifteen

As the hours pass on Monday on the ledge, Jake's sister, Anne, who was expecting Jake to call Sunday was growing anxious about her brother. Knowing if she doesn't hear from him by tonight, she will start calling around, since his phone goes directly to voice mail. At 10:00 P.M., Anne, who hasn't heard from Jake, calls Kayla in California. "Hi, Kayla. It's Anne. How are you?, Anne asked. "I'm good, Anne. How are you? And how's Jack? I miss you guys", she replies. "We miss you too. Listen, have you heard from Jake?", asks Anne. "Hmmm. We'd been texting but I haven't heard back from him since like Friday night. Is everything okay?, Kayla asked. Anne then asked, "did he tell you where he was going?" Kayla replied "No. He just said he was going away skiing for a few days. Wherever he was we texted Friday night. I guess the people in the room next to him were pretty active, if you know what I mean, but I haven't heard from him since."

Anne said, "if you hear from him, please tell him to call me. I'm worried. This isn't like him. When he says he's going to do something, he does it. I know he's a big boy, but he's the only family I have. He's my little brother. Jack and I would be devastated if anything happened to him."

"Okay, Anne", exclaimed Kayla, "and vice versa if you hear from him. Please let me know. I know he's been through a lot, but you're right, it's not like him. Have you tried calling him?" "Yes", replied Anne, "it goes right to voice mail." Kayla says "please let me know, okay?" Anne replied, "I will. Take care. Bye." Anne hung up the phone. She called a couple of Jake's friends only to hear they hadn't talked to him in a week and neither were aware he even went away.

Anne didn't sleep all night. Getting up early on Tuesday morning, and getting Jake's voice mail once again, she knew she had to do something before Jack got up. She called the Boston police.

The dispatcher answered. "Boston Police. How may I direct your call?" Ann replied, "I need to speak to someone. My brother's missing." The dispatcher asked how long he'd been missing. Anne knew it had to be more than a couple of days, so she replied "since Friday, sir".

"Is that when you last saw or spoke to him", the dispatcher asked.

"Yes, sir", Anne replied.

"Have you checked around to see if anyone had contact with him," the dispatcher asked.

"Yes, sir. I've done all that and he was supposed to call me Sunday and his phone goes right to voice mail", Ann replied.

"Did he go away for work?"

"No, Friday was his last day on his job but he didn't go. He took off to go skiing."

"He told you he was going skiing?, the dispatcher asked.

"Yes, he got his severance. So much has happened these last few months. He didn't tell anyone where he was going."

"What do you mean so much has happened?", the dispatcher asked.

"Well first our dad died. Then his girlfriend got a job in California and moved out there. Lastly, his job was eliminated and he was let go."

"Wow, ma'am, that's a lot to put on anyone's plate. I'm sorry to hear that. Your brother wasn't suicidal was he?", the dispatcher asked.

"Absolutely not!", Anne replied emphatically.

"I'm sorry, ma'am, but I have to ask."

"I know. I'm sorry I snapped. I'm just worried about him and afraid to tell my son. Jake is like a father to Jack".

"Why don't you come down to the station and fill out a missing person's report and we'll go from there."

"Okay, officer. Thank you. What is your name, sir?", Anne asked.

"Officer O'Brien", he replied.

"Thank you again. I'll see you soon", Anne said.

When Jack got up Anne told him they had to go to the police station and talk to an officer. Jack said "Okay. Can I look at a police car?"

Ann said, "sure you can, Jack. I'd love to show you a police car. Maybe an officer will let you look inside. Who knows, they might let you sit in one".

"That would be cool", said Jack.

Jack and Anne went down to the precinct so she could fill out the report. An officer kept Jack busy while Anne did the paperwork and answered questions. While they were finishing up, Anne noticed two nicely dressed men were standing there. One was holding a tv camera, the other had a briefcase. The man with the briefcase said "excuse me. I couldn't help but overhear you talking about a missing person". Anne's eyes immediately started to well up. Her lip was quivering when she replied "my brother is missing". The man said, "we are from WBV. We're here to cover another story, but we would very much like to do a story on your brother if that's okay. It could help you find him." Anne broke down, but fought back the tears not wanting Jack to see she was upset. She agreed to do the story, and the officer with Jack took him out to see a police car.

When the interview was over, the anchorman said "we will air this on the six o'clock news tonight so if anyone has any information on your brother's whereabouts, hopefully they will come forward". "Thank you so much", Anne said.

# Chapter Sixteen

Tuesday night at six o'clock while Jake is still stranded on the ledge inside the cave, unbeknownst to him a missing person story is about to air on WBV. He lay there cuddled up with Jack the bear, a bottle of water and a somber mood that with every passing hour knowing he will not last much longer. The cold, his knee, and loneliness are taking a toll on him mentally and physically.

At the same time in Manchester, New Hampshire, after having dinner with his family, Tim Chandler sits down to watch the news and read the paper. Looking at the paper as the news comes on, Tim hears the story of how this Boston man has been missing since Friday. He puts the paper down in time to see Jake's face big as life on the tv in his livingroom.

"That's Jake!", he screams. His wife comes running in from the kitchen. "Honey, that's Jake! The guy who gave me a ride Friday when my car broke down! He's missing! How can he be missing? Oh, that's right. He said nobody knew where he was going."

"He didn't tell anyone? That's not very smart", his wife replied.

"That's not the point. If you knew what he had been through, you'd want to get away too. I envy what he was doing. I need to call the number", Tim said. He grabs his phone and dials the number on the bottom of the screen. He gets an answer.

"WBV Tip Line. What can I do for you?"

"Hi. My name is Tim Chandler from Manchester, New Hampshire. The guy, Jake Christopher that's missing, you just aired the story, he went skiing at Killington, Vermont. The story said he went skiing and nobody knew where. He picked me up Friday morning when I was having car trouble. He brought me to the VA in White River Junction and was then headed for Killington. He didn't have any reservations, but I know that's where he was headed. He said he would find a room. Yes, I'll give you my information, but you have to find him and let me know when you do."

"Sir, this is a Tip Line. We take information and pass it on", said the lady on the other end.

"I'm sorry, ma'am. I just want to know if he's okay."

"I understand, Mr. Chandler. I'm passing on your information. Someone may call you for more information, so is this the best number to call?"

"Yes it is", Tim replied.

"Okay. Thank you for calling the WBV Tip Line. Have a nice evening".

Tim, pacing back and forth in his living room says to his wife, "Jake is such a nice guy. I hope this is all a misunderstanding and it's just because nobody knew where he went."

"I'm sure that's what it is. You shouldn't go places without communicating with someone", Tim's wife said.

"It's a long story, honey, but let me tell you, he had reasons", Tim said.

The Tip Line acted immediately on Tim's tip. They called Anne.

"Hello? Anne Christopher?

"Yes", she replied.

"We had a call on the Tip Line that your brother may have gone to Killington, Vermont skiing."

Anne quickly replied "I know he has skied there before"

"We're going to alert the authorities in Killington. Do you know the make, model and plate number of his car?"

"It's a black BMW X5 with open ski racks on the roof. I don't know his plate number."

"We will pass this on to the Boston PD. They can find out the plate number and they will alert the authorities in Killington. Ms. Christopher..."

"Yes", Anne replied.

"Good luck. I hope they find your brother."

Anne's eyes well up again. "So do I, so do I. Thank you."

Boston PD, through the DMV, locates Jake's license plate number and calls the authorities in Killington. "We have a tip that we received that a missing person could possibly have gone to Killington skiing Friday. His family hasn't heard from him and frankly didn't know where he was until a tip came in on the WBV Tip Line that aired on the six o'clock news. Apparently he went up there with no reservation but claimed he would find a room. So that would definitely mean a hotel and not a condo."

"Okay, Boston, thank you. We will check all hotels for the subject's car. Thanks for the information. We will let you know if we find anything".

"Okay. Good luck", replied Boston PD.

Killington PD in turn alerts the Sheriff's Department that they may need help in searching for the subject's vehicle at 8:00 P.M. At 10:00 P.M. a Rutland County sheriff pulls into the Fountain Inn parking lot. Checking all the vehicles in the front, he proceeds to drive around back. He locates a black BMW X5 covered with snow. He verifies the plate to be Jake's car and calls it into his dispatch.

The sheriff then goes to the front desk to see if Jake is a registered guest at the Inn. The clerk confirms he is registered there and has booked the room until tomorrow. "Can you get a key to his room and lead me there, please", the sheriff asked. "Sure", said the clerk.

They go down the small flight of stairs and to the right. At the door they discover the Do Not Disturb sign. The clerk knocks and hollers "Mr. Christopher. This is the front desk". "Knock louder", the sheriff says. So the clerk knocks louder and repeats what he said.

The sheriff says to the clerk "we need to open the door. Since we aren't sure what we'll find, I better do it." "Okay with me", says the clerk. The sheriff opened the door and flips on the light. The room is just the way Jake left it. The sheriff checks the bathroom just to be sure. "Somebody has definitely been here, but they aren't now. It would be nice to ask the neighboring guests if they'd seen anything", said the sheriff.

The clerk agreed to knock on doors. There was no answer at the first one, so they try another. The lady that smokes next door answered. The sheriff said "sorry to bother you, but have you seen anyone come and go from that room since you've been here?" The lady said "I saw the guy that was in there Friday night. Dinner was the last time I saw him. I haven't heard anything from over there either. I thought he may have checked out and forgot to pull the Do Not Disturb sign off the door."

"Okay, thank you. Sorry to bother you", said the sheriff.

"That's okay", the lady said as she closed the door.

The sheriff said to the clerk, "Okay. His ski equipment isn't in the room or his car. His keys were on the table. His car hasn't been moved since before it snowed. He's either staying with someone else, or he's up on the mountain". The clerk just nodded in agreement. "What should we do?", asks the clerk.

"I need to call my superior, but it looks to me like we need to organize a search and rescue", said the sheriff. They headed back to the front desk. The sheriff went back out to his car. He came back in several minutes later and said, "we're organizing a search and rescue for the first thing in the morning. It will be in the parking lot across the road".

"Okay. I have already emailed all employees that a guest is missing. We will cooperate fully", said the clerk.

In the meantime, the Killington PD reported back to the Boston PD that they had located the subject's vehicle and are treating it as a missing person, most likely lost on the mountain. In turn the Boston PD called Anne with the news. "We assure you, Ms. Christopher, that there is hope now. We know where he is. We just need to find him." Relieved and grateful for the news, Anne asked "how did you find where he was so fast?" The officer replied "I can't tell you who, but your brother helped somebody along the way and they saw the story. They called immediately and we found his car at a hotel at ten o'clock this evening."

"That's my brother", Anne said, "he would help a stranger."

"That's what happened", said the officer, "sounds like a special guy. I hope we find him."

"Me too", said Anne.

Anne hung up the phone and as much as she hated to, she had to wake Jack and head to Killington. Her brother needed her and he needed Jack. There was no way she could leave him behind. Before waking Jack, Anne called Kayla to tell her the news. "I'm headed up there. I don't know much yet, but I'll keep you informed." Kayla didn't know what to make of it and felt helpless, but knew Jake was capable of surviving anything. After all he had been through, she believed in him more than anyone.

# Chapter Seventeen

Anne and Jack arrived at the Fountain Inn at 3:00 A.M. The clerk who was still on duty greeted them as though they were guests. Through his compassion and empathy, he offered to let Anne and Jack who was asleep in her arms, have Jake's room to rest until the search party was to form at 7:00 A.M.

Anne, overwhelmed with the whole ordeal, tears streaming down her face, accepted the kind gesture and walked with him to the stairway and Jake's room. First, the clerk pointed out the entrance to show her Jake's vehicle still covered in snow. Then unlocked the door to his room, and as she entered she knew for sure this was his room.

She laid Jack on the unmade bed. She saw how he had things laid out that he didn't wear. She picked up the tissue with two fingers and dropped it in the trash can, not wanting to know what it was. She then thanked the clerk and when he asked if he could get her anything, she said, "no. Thank you. You've already done enough".

She took off her coat and laid down next to Jack and immediately drifted off to sleep. At 6:30 A.M. she awoke, jumped up and freshened up as best she could. She used Jake's stuff he had laid out on the sink to at least have a respectable appearance.

The clerk was still there so he could be of any assistance when the search party formed, and to offer any information they may need. Anne went up to the front desk to ask for a door key so that she could leave Jack in the room knowing he wouldn't wake up until at least 7:30 A.M. Not only did the clerk offer her a key, he also offered to have a female employee who was due to come in soon stay with Jack so he wouldn't wake up alone. The clerk knew Anne would be right across the road and Anne agreed that it was a good idea. She can be by Jack's side in sixty seconds if she needed to. She gave the clerk her cell number to give to the female employee when Jack woke up, or to call for any reason at all.

It wasn't even 7:00 A.M. and dozens of vehicles had already arrived in the parking lot. Anne was there to greet those that were heading up the operation. At 7:00 A.M. it's starting to get light and off in the distance you could hear the sound of a helicopter closing in. Seconds later the flashing lights became visible. They all watched in awe at the size of this military copter that was landing in the parking lot. As the propeller slows and the engine winds down, four men jump out as the chopper sits idling. They join about fifty others who are either police, fire, foresters, military, ski patrol, and good Samaritans who want to help find this missing person.

In a giant circle they agree to start searching right here on the mountain in front of us, between Snowshed and Ramshead. The skiers in the group are going to ski the edges to see if he just veered off and is lying injured where he couldn't be seen. Some others are searching on snowmobile, some on foot.

At 7:30 A.M. the group disperses to head out on their assignments. As the chopper takes flight and flies off over Snowshed Lodge to make its way up the mountain, Anne decides she needs to check on Jack. She walks back into the hotel. The clerk says to the young girl with him, "this is the mother of the little boy. Anne, this is Amanda. Amanda, Anne. Amanda just got here Anne, so I just started telling her what was going on. Amanda said "I'm very sorry to hear about your brother. I hope they find him quickly."

"Thank you. So do I", said Anne. She then said to Amanda, let's go check on Jack. I'll introduce you if he's awake. I'd like to bounce back and forth so I can get updates on the search if you don't mind hanging with Jack some." "I would love to", said Amanda.

As they headed down the stairs, Amanda asked how long had her brother been missing. "Since Saturday", Anne replied. When Anne stopped at Room 103, Amanda screamed loudly.

"What's the matter", asked Anne. Amanda crying said, "what's your brother's name".

"Jake", she replied.

"Oh my God, oh my God, oh my God. Jake was in room 103. Jake is missing?, Amanda asked.

"How do you know Jake?"

"I rented him the room."

"Are you the girl he asked out, but you left because your brother had an accident?, Anne asked.

"Yes!", Amanda said helplessly.

"Oh my", said Anne, "Jake was hurt but trust me, he believed you. Is your brother okay?", Anne asked.

"Yes. He'll be okay. He was in the hospital for a couple of days, but he'll recover, replied Amanda. "Anne, I am so sorry. I ran out of the restaurant when I got the call about my brother. Jake and I were going to go out for a drink. We never exchanged numbers. I was late getting here Saturday and we didn't see each other. I have Sunday's and Monday's off. Jake rented the room for Friday and Saturday night. I assumed he left on Sunday. Apparently at some point he must have gone and extended his stay. Anne said. I just assumed he left. I never looked at the schedule". Replied Amanda.

"It's okay, dear. He will forgive you", Anne said.

"I hope so. Please, they have to find him", exclaimed Amanda.

# Chapter Eighteen

Meanwhile, Jake is trying to muster up the energy to go out and repack the water bottle. Even though he was cuddled up with Jack, he was freezing. His knee was as tight as could be, sore as hell, and it hurt to move it. All he wanted to do was lie still. Any movement hurt. It's 10:00 A.M. and he remembers his father's words "if you give up, he will understand". Either way, I win, he thought.

Soon after that, he hears something, it's the sound of a helicopter. It's getting closer and closer. He wiggles and worms his head to the entrance, his limp body behind him. He sees the most beautiful sight he has ever seen. The helicopter is hovering in front of his skis. "Hey!" He pokes an arm out. "I'm here, I'm here!" The men in the helicopter wave back. He lays his head down, tears streaming off his cheeks. He looks back into the cave "we did it, Jack, we did it!"

Inside the helicopter the pilot radios the folks at the command post. "We found a pair of skis crossed on a ledge in the snow. Our guy poked his head out of a tiny cave. We found him! I repeat, we found him, he's alive! We are just up over the top on the southwest side. We'll repel down with a board and grab him. He appears to be injured, but we can get him. I'm not sure how he got here, but we sure are happy to see him. Over!"

Inside the Inn, Anne, Jack and Amanda are in Jake's room when there's a knock on the door. The motel manager is standing there with a huge grin on his face and says "they found him. He's alive! He's alive!" They both screamed and hugged. They grabbed Jack and ran out to the command post. There it was confirmed that he's alive. They are flying him straight to the hospital.

At that moment they were elated that he survived, but neither of them could wait to see him. Amanda got permission to go with Anne and Jack to the hospital. Amanda barely knows Jake but she felt like she needed a second chance. She had spent the last few hours with Anne and Jack and in that time had gained so much respect for the man she only knew as Jake in Room 103.    On the way to the hospital, while Amanda drove, Anne texted Kayla and told her Jake was found and is okay. She replied that that was wonderful, that she knew Jake would be okay and would text him later.

When they arrive at the emergency room, the men who found him were leaving the hospital walking back out to the helicopter. The two women and little boy walked up to them and Jack said "are you the pilots from the helicopter that found my Uncle Jake?" They chuckled and replied "yes".

"Thank you", said Jack.

"You're welcome, son. Are you Jack?", the pilot asked.

"Yes", said Jack.

The pilot knelt down and put his hands on Jack's shoulders. "We rescued him, but you saved him" and gave Jack a hug. The ladies hugged them as well then ran into the emergency entrance past a huge crowd and a slew of media.

The doctors and nurses were all around him so Jake couldn't be seen. Anne said to a nurse, "I'm his sister. When can I see him?" The nurse replied "we are doing an evaluation. I'll ask the doctor when one comes out." Several minutes later a doctor emerges and the nurse points to Anne as she speaks to him.

The doctor walked over and said "Hi. I'm Dr. Santiago. You are Jake's sister?" "Yes", Anne said. The doctor asks "and she is?" Without hesitation, Anne said "that's his girlfriend Amanda". Amanda chuckled and nodded her head. The doctor replied "then I can speak with you both".

The doctor reports, "Jake is overall okay. He does have a severe leg injury. I've ordered an MRI to find out the extent. Surprisingly enough, having spent four days on top of a mountain in mostly below freezing temperatures, he's lucky he doesn't have frostbite. He has quite a remarkable story. Would you like to see him?"

"Yes, please", Anne said.

"Okay, one at a time", the doctor said.

"You go first", said Amanda.

"Thank you", Anne replied with a chuckle. "I'll tell him someone else is here to see him. He's going to love seeing you. I know it."

"I hope so", Amanda replied.

Anne walked in and peeked in the curtain. "Hey you little brat. How are you doing?"

"Anne, I'm so glad to see you."

"How do you feel?", Anne asked.

"As you can see, for the most part I'm fine, but I trashed my left knee. I can't even budge it. I think I tore everything in it that could rip. It's the most excruciating pain I've ever felt".

"You're alive, that's what matters. I have Jack in the waiting room, but he's not allowed in. There is someone else out there who would like to say hello to you", replied Anne.

"Okay, but tell Jack I've missed him, that I love him and that he saved me. I mean it. Please tell him."

Anne replied "that's what the pilot said as well. What do you mean Jack saved you?"

"Remember when I wanted to talk to Jack Saturday morning and you wouldn't wake him because you said he'd be a bear if you did?"

"Yeah?"

"When I crashed on the ledge, not only did I tear my knee up, but when I crawled into the cave for cover, there was a hibernating bear inside."

"Get out!", Anne said.

"I'm not lying! I named him Jack. Not only that, I packed my water bottle with snow, put it under his armpit and the heat melted the snow so I had water to drink. I cuddled with it for heat and I talked his fucking ear off. Jack saved my life."

"This is an incredible story! I have an incredible story for you too!", Anne said.

"Oh yeah, it can't beat mine".

Anne disappeared. In the next instant Jake hears "hello, Jake. Do you remember me?" In walks Amanda and his jaw drops.

"Oh my God! Amanda!" He reached out his hands, Amanda takes his and Jake says "how is your brother?" Her eyes sparkled with tears and says "he's okay. He's recovering but he's okay. He spent two days in the hospital. He got pretty banged up, but I don't want to talk about him."

"How did you know this happened. How did you end up with Anne?"

"Long story. I'll tell you about it some time. I just want you to know I wanted to go have that drink with you, but I got the call about my brother. I had to go", Amanda explained.

"I understand. I knew you had an emergency. But I'm so glad you're here now. I have a question for Anne I need the answer to".

"One second", said Amanda, as she exited.

Anne came in "what is it?"

"How did you find out where I was? Nobody knew."

"You hadn't called me like you promised. I got worried and filed a missing person's report. While I was at the Boston PD filing the report, WBV was there. They overheard my story and asked to interview me. I gave them a picture of you and they did a story on the six o'clock news. Some guy you helped on your way to Vermont saw the newscast and called", Anne explained.

"Tim, he saved my life?"

"I have an idea. I'll be back. I'm sending Amanda back in", Anne said.

Anne went out and called the reporter who did the story from WBV. She told him all about the recovery operation and thanked him. She then said "can you do me one more favor?

"I'll try", he said.

"Can you air on the six o'clock news that they found Jake because of last night's story? I'm hoping the man, his name is Tim, sees it and knows he saved Jake's life. He deserves to know," Anne said.

"I'll work it in somehow. Thanks for the update. This is truly front page news that rarely makes the front page", the reporter said.

"Thank you", said Anne. "I have to get back to my brother".

Anne went to the front desk. "Can I bring my son in with me to see Jake. He would love to see Jack", Anne asked.

"I'm sorry, ma'am. They are ready to do Jake's MRI. We'll see about that when he returns. Just then Amanda came out. She was gleaming from ear to ear.

Amanda said "he is such a good guy. They are taking him for his MRI. He said he'll be back shortly. He showed me the goodbye messages he recorded before his phone died. A nurse charged his phone for him. It melted my heart.

Anne said, "I can't believe he slept with a bear"

"Huh? He didn't say anything about a bear. Besides showing me his goodbye messages, all he talked about was Jack, and how all he could think about was that he promised to never let him down", Amanda explained.

"That doesn't surprise me", Anne said with a smile. "The media are chomping at the bit to interview him. We may have to give them some time if Jake is ready to speak."

"You're right", said Amanda. "We'll see if he's ready after the MRI".

Jake came back from the MRI and told his nurse that he needs to see his nephew. The nurses let Jack in while they prepare a room for him.

"Uncle Jake", Jack hollered and ran to his bed. "I missed you", he exclaimed. Jake lifted him onto his right side of the bed and winced.

"Are you okay, Uncle Jake?" Jack said. "I am now little buddy. I'm going to tell you all about how you saved my life.

"I did?", Jack asked.

As Anne and Amanda looked through the glass, they were both smiling. The media behind them in the emergency room entrance were pleading with the nurses for their turn to interview Jake.

In the meantime, WBV is preparing to work in the recovery story for the six o'clock news. Tim had gone to work that morning and told everyone, including Mr. White, that the man who gave him a ride to the meeting at the VA was missing and nobody knew where he was until Tim called the tip line. Still worried about his friend, Tim sat down to watch the news as he had done the night before, as did all of his colleagues, including Mr. White.

The news came on with the announcement that Jake had been found because of a tip from the segment the night before. Tim raised both of his arms and jumped up and down and screamed "he's alive!" In fact, everyone he worked with was watching and knew it was Tim's phone call that led to his recovery. Mr. White couldn't have been more proud of Tim, and was grateful for Jake's survival.

# Chapter Nineteen

Back at the hospital, Jake had received the results from the MRI. He, Anne, Amanda and Jack were in his room discussing the grim results when his phone rang.

"Hello, Mr. Christopher. This is the operator. We have an outside call for you."

"Who is it?", asked Jake.

"His name is Tim Chandler, sir", the operator said.

Jake in amazement said "yes, please put him through."

"Okay, sir".

Jake put his hand over the receiver and announced with excitement that Tim is on the phone.

"Hello, Tim! I'm so glad you called. Thank you, my friend. I don't know how I can ever repay you". Tim joked, "I felt the same way, I guess we are even." Their conversation was like two old friends who were just getting caught up on life.

Jake's demeanor did a quick 180 when Tim asked what his prognosis was. "Well, Tim", said Jake, "my knee is completely tore up. I tore the ACL, MCL, and PCL. I shattered my kneecap. The doc says he's never seen anything like it. He has to confer with several specialists to figure out what to do.

Tim was quick to respond. He simply said, "Jake, you'll be okay. Don't worry about what you don't know. Doctors are amazing when they put their heads together".

"I know", said Jake. Like I told you before, I've never suffered a serious injury".

"I remember", said Tim. "Keep your chin up and stay positive".

"Thanks, Tim. I don't know how I could ever repay you", said Jake.

"You don't owe me anything", said Tim. "Just stay positive and do what you need to do to get better. Thanks again, my friend, for giving me the ride to the VA. The meeting was a huge success."

"I'm glad", said Jake. "Your business card is still in my car at the hotel. I was going to call as soon as I could".

"I beat you to it", chuckled Tim, "Take care. We'll talk soon".

The next morning Jake lay alone in his room at 10:00 A.M. Anne, Jack and Amanda had gone to retrieve his car and clean out his room. He heard a knock on his door. "Come in", said Jake. The door opens slowly and Tim pokes his head in. "Oh my God! Tim! What are you doing here? I can't believe you came to see me!"

Tim said "I had to. I couldn't wait to see you, and what I have to say couldn't wait either". Jake looked puzzled and said "what do you mean? What do you have to say?"

"Well, my friend, after I got off the phone with you last night I called my boss and told him all about you and your knee. Mr. White would be honored if you agreed to be the first recipient of our knee replacement prototype. He is prepared to cover the cost of everything, including rehab." Jake looked like he just saw a ghost. He opened his mouth and nothing came out.

Tim said "that's not all". Jake was barely able to mutter "what?" "Mr. White wants to offer you a job at the company when you recover. He said he would be honored to have you as part of our family. He will even pay to move you to Manchester. We would work together. You and I would be a team. I told you Mr. White is a great boss!"

Jake sat there in awe and put his arms out as he embraced the idea and screamed "yes, I accept all of it!" Tim leaned over and hugged his new colleague.

When Anne and Amanda came back, Jake told them the incredible news. The joy in the room was unimaginable. From his hospital bed Jake devised a plan. With the help from volunteers who had heard his amazing story of how a hibernating bear named Jack saved his life, a team of specialists descended onto the ledge and left a smorgasbord of food outside the cave. When Jack wakes up from his long winter's nap he doesn't have to wander around all groggy-like looking for food. His finishing touch was to hang a sign above the opening that said "Jack". He only wished he could watch his friend emerge from the cave in the spring.

One year after the accident, Jake's knee has fully recovered. He is at work full time. He loves his new job and working with Tim. On Saturday morning the last weekend in January a year to the day, the alarm goes off at 6:00 AM. Jake shuts off the alarm, rolls over and wraps his arms around Amanda. He whispers in her ear, "happy anniversary. It was a year ago today we met. That day I was searching for myself and I found you, I never want to let you go, you make me so happy".

He rolls over and opens the drawer on his night stand and pulls out a box. He gets out of bed as she climbs to his side of the bed. He gets down on his new knee and says, "Amanda a year ago I had lost everything. What a difference a year makes, now I have everything. You have made me the luckiest guy on earth, will you marry me?" Amanda was gleaming and said, "on one condition?" Jake smiled and said, "of course it's a different ring." "Then yes" said Amanda. "I will marry you!" He put the ring on her finger, looked her in the eyes and gave her a big kiss and then a hug. As he is hugging her, he looks over at the same picture of his dad who now has a smile on his face.

The end.